# DEAHN BERRINI

## MILKWEED: A NOVEL

# DEAHN BERRINI

# MILKWEED
# A NOVEL

**SOMERSET HALL PRESS**
Boston, Massachusetts

Published by Somerset Hall Press
416 Commonwealth Avenue, Suite 612
Boston, Massachusetts 02215
www.somersethallpress.com

ISBN: 978-1-935244-01-1



Library of Congress Cataloging-in-Publication Data
Berrini, Deahn.
  Milkweed : a novel / Deahn Berrini.
      p. cm.
  ISBN 978-1-935244-01-1 (pbk.)
  1. Young women--Fiction. 2. North Shore (Mass. : Coast)--
Fiction. I. Title.
  PS3602.E76358M55 2009
  813'.6--dc22                                    2008054399

In Memory Of
Kathleen Wilkinson

## April 12, 1956

The yellow kitchen gathers light.

The last memory Cassie has of her mother is in this yellow kitchen. Gold specks sparkle on the linoleum and buttercups sway on the curtains over the window. They are making breakfast and, in the morning sun, every corner is sharp, every color bright. Her mother, a hazy figure with soft brown hair and bustle, carries over the eggs.

Cassie lines the eggs up to take their places into the blue glass bowl. "March!" she commands. Sent off kilter, they roll one by one off the counter onto the floor. She climbs down from her chair, but as she scoops up the shifting mass of clear and orange-yellow, the misshapen gel slips through her fingers. She starts to cry.

Her mother presses the tears away from her face with the flat of her thumbs, presses her in a warm hug. "Shh, shh, Cassandra. Eggs break. Things break."

As if she knew that within the morning a drunk would speed down Route 1 on the wrong side of the road and plow into her car so that there was never a chance she'd survive the impact of the crash.


Fifteen years separate that morning from this, a sunny May morning with a warm wind that blows in the windows Cassie has opened.

### May 29, 1971

Cassie's father sits at the kitchen table in his worn, backless house slippers, drinking coffee over the sports page. When Cassie returns from the mailbox and opens the back door, the breeze rattles the sides of her father's paper.

"I don't care how much that boy can hit," comments her dad, a lean man with quiet eyes, "that Yaz is still a cold fish."

"Mark is coming home." She stands reading over the counter, head down, loose brown hair falling forward.

Her dad squints up at her. Thin and dark, she looks nothing like her mother did. People who meant well looked for the resemblance, but Frank Leahy isn't a man who places fat bets on thin hopes.

"He's being pulled out on Tuesday. Then he's being sent home on Thursday." Mark has been in Vietnam for over eleven months.

"Thank God," says Frank. His choice of words strikes her because, unless you count the Red Sox, her father is not a religious man.

Cassie refolds the slight airmail paper into a neat rectangle and slips the envelope into the rear pocket of her jeans. She remembers two years ago when Mark had come, white faced and silent, draft notice in hand to this same kitchen. The news had shocked Cassie into silence, but her father had sat Mark down. "Do you know why you're fighting?" he had asked.

"The communists."

"Who are the communists?"

But Mark had come around to a decision, "Mr. Leahy," and he'd looked at Cassie as he spoke, "I don't want to be a Canadian. I want to be American."

The wind shuffles her father's paper, shifts Cassie back to the present. "Is everything all right?" her dad asks.

Of course it is. But the well of relief feels surrounded by wild nerves. Cassie takes Mark's letter out of her pocket to look again at the reassuring precision of his handwriting. Mark is coming home in one piece; this is the moment she's hoped for. She smiles at her father.

Frank doesn't return the smile. "Isn't his tour only over next week?"

Cassie glances at the clock on the stove. Low tide is an hour gone and she needs to get to work. "I guess they don't waste any time."

Her dad doesn't return to his paper. "Be careful, Cassie."

"I've got to get to work." She kisses the side of his face, above the cheek and close to the temple, where the blood flows thin below his skin.

Cassie takes her bike from where it leans in the grass against the back of the house and scans the yard. She and her father are not gardeners, and their backyard is an un-cultivated no-man's-land that stretches ten yards to the old northbound tracks, long overgrown with weeds since service beyond Ipswich stopped years ago. The new shoots are small, green and wet in the bright sunshine. By full summer, this patch will be wild and overgrown with plants that Mark had identified for her.

The first plant he'd named grew in a patch, had thick stems that bled milk if broken and produced sturdy sacs that went from summer green to hard brown in the late fall. As a small girl, she had cracked open these thick, brown sacs to release the feathery wisps hidden within; each strand carried a wee brown seed that trailed in the wind like an upside-down kite. Years later, after she'd grown and met Mark, they'd found themselves in her yard, and he'd pointed to a plant and said,

"Hey, that's milkweed." She'd laughed nervously at first, thinking he was joking like so many other boys, but he'd held her wrist in the most delicate way and pulled her to a patch of plants with broad leaves. Kneeling, he'd folded a leaf carefully back. It had rained and his pants were damp. "Look," he'd whispered. "Under here, this tiny white egg."

Cassie had barely distinguished the white dot from the creamy veins of the leaf. "What is it?"

He'd snapped the leaf from the stem and handed it to her. "I'm not going to tell you. You're going to have to feed it to find out. But I'll give you a hint. All it eats are milkweed leaves."

Mark, who knew the names of hundreds of plants and tress, once wrote to her: "Everything's oversized here, freaky and huge and growing feet overnight, and I don't know the name of one goddamned thing."

He has written hundreds of letters to her over the last two years; they come every couple of days or so, or in clumps of four sometimes, but it has been a long time since she's seen him, a long time since he's seen the landscape he could name so easily. Cassie blinks in the sun and turns the bike out of the driveway and heads to work.

Cosmo Shellfish Company lies a half-mile from the Leahy home, across the tracks, housed in a refrigerated Quonset hut that was transplanted after World War II from a base in southern New Hampshire by a Cosmo cousin with a flatbed truck. After four years of working at Cosmo, Cassie has heard and reheard all the stories, and, like Homer, old man Cosmo hung his tales onto the minute hooks of lineage. "It was my mother's second cousin on her father's side," this one began, "although his family had come here just before the war." The old man raised his palms slightly at this point in the telling. "Why spend money on a new building when one comes for free on the back of a truck?"

Cassie parks her bike against the metal siding, in the shade and out of the way of the loading zone. As she enters the refrigerated hut, she's temporarily blinded after the bright spring sunshine. Shivering, she heads for the anteroom next to the office, grabs a navy blue sweatshirt off a hook, pulls the hood over her head, and shoves her hands into the front pockets. Somewhere in the whir of the refrigeration, she hears the whoosh of the hose. Someone else must be washing down the loading area in anticipation of the fresh catch, which the clammers will bring in as soon as the rising tide covers the flats. In the office, Cassie picks up Monday's delivery sheet to tally how many bushels of shucked clams will be needed to fill the orders. The numbers soothe her, Mark's letter forgotten for a few brief moments, but then the phone rings, and Cassie starts, her nerves jangled. She picks up the receiver.

"Cosmo Shellfish."

Old man Cosmo himself appears in the doorway. A broad-shouldered man with a deeply lined face, he smiles to see Cassie on the phone and disappears into the murky whir that lies beyond the brightly lit office.

It's a chef from the city looking for mussels. "We don't have any," she tells him. And we won't ever, she could have added, because old man Cosmo doesn't like change, and his nephew, George, takes after his uncle. Still, she takes down the message and leaves it in the clear plastic file cemented to the wall, with the name "George" printed on it in large block letters. Next to George's hangs another labeled "Cosmo" and more recently, one labeled "David."

As Cassie tallies the bushels, she puts on the coffee. The rich odor fills the small room and the quiet gurgle of the machine focuses her on the task at hand and not out toward the bays and the constant noise of the refrigerators. She searches for stray messages, receipts, and orders; despite George's hard nose for business, neither he nor old man Cosmo has any patience for paper.

Neither did Mark, really, until he went away. He was always most comfortable outdoors. Then the letters came, sometimes every day, and had kept coming. They overran her nightstand and several shoeboxes under her bed. Now when she thinks of him, she thinks of the way he looked and made her feel before he left, or what he's written and shared since, as if Mark were split in two, like the Asian symbol where the white curls around the black like a snake, but they never meet to gray. Will the two parts of Mark come together when he comes home to be someone she doesn't recognize? Or someone who is no longer interested in her?

The coffee burps, the cycle finished. Why waste her time with useless questions? Cassie pours two cups, one black, one with sugar and cream and brings them out to old man Cosmo and George, who are standing outside the "B" unit that runs too cold on a regular basis. Cosmo Shellfish sells fresh seafood, not frozen, and the unit's created its share of trouble over the last several months. George has a wrench in one hand and the temperature gauge in the other. He drops both to take his coffee.

"I just got another call in for mussels," she tells them.

"Peasant food," smiles Cosmo as he receives his warm cup. "They're not tender enough, like the soft shells."

"How many?" asks George.

"Not too many," Cassie admits. "Forty pounds."

George sips his coffee. He and his uncle are made of circles. With their broad round shoulders, global bellies, deep grooves aside mouths, and strong legs close to the ground, they lack the sharp edges that snag, the angles that irritate.

In the back, Cassie hears the hose turn off. A truck rolls over the gravel outside in the lot beyond the receiving bay, the first of the clammers to pull up and unload. Her hand reaches back to touch the pocket that contains her letter and then forward to pull the hood off her head. She's too warm in the thick sweatshirt. With three people here, she won't be needed for the receiving, or the setup for the next shucking. "I'm gonna do the paperwork today," she tells them, and George nods as he puts his coffee down and picks up the wrench.

Light streams in from the large, side door. "Hey beautiful," a large, dark man in a checkered flannel shirt calls to her. "Ya gonna check the freight?"

Cassie waves an arm. "No, Freddo, not me today."

"You know, Cassie," he says, cursing between breaths as he gently sets an overladen burlap sack onto the cement floor. "That boyfriend of yours better get back soon, or you'll be taken!"

Cassie slows her step and touches her back pocket. "He's being shipped home," she calls back, her voice casual as her face flushes hot. Why was it so warm in here today? "I just heard."

"No shit," says Freddo.

"Cassie!" Old man Cosmo, still holding the coffee cup, comes up to her, and stands, almost as if he's pausing before a formal speech. She can't look at him, glances toward the open door, and then is blinded by the light so that when she looks back at the old man, he's covered in tiny stars. "Is everything all right with him?"

"Yes, they just send them all right home when their tour is over, no waiting." She backs away from the questions toward the office.

"Good," says Cosmo and smiles into his own pause. "He's home now."

"That's great," calls George over the open engine of the generator. "That's great news."

As Cassie retreats over the office threshold, she turns and sees a mass of dark brown curls and long arms that end in longer fingers. She glances away again. Although she hasn't seen him in months, it's David Cosmo, bent over the safe.

She knew he was here when she heard the water rushing out of the hose down the drains. Her stomach curls tight into a ball, and she feels pulled like a piece of driftwood in an undertow. "Hi," she says quickly.

Caught by surprise, David's partly open mouth and inquiring eyes briefly remind Cassie of a baby bird who only expects his mother with a fat worm. Then he quickly stands.

"Cassie, do you happen to know the new combination? I'm doing the receiving and my father must have changed it again."

David graduated college this spring. Cassie has been expecting to run into him ever since the plastic folder bearing his name appeared on the wall a week or so ago, but George must have sent him down to New Bedford to check on the scallop boats. For most of last summer, David had been out checking boats, or digging himself, never around the office. Since old man Cosmo had only daughters and they'd both married accountants, David, as expected, must have decided to go into the family business.

Cassie could tell David that George changes the combination twice a year, March 25 and October 26, Greek Independence Day and the anniversary of his father's death, your grandfather, Nicolas Cosmo, co-founder of Cosmo Shellfish Company, and that he changed it over two months ago.

"Sometimes it's cranky," she says and kneels down to work the lock. "Three-twenty-five-twenty-six. Don't write it down," she adds as she pulls out the zippered canvas bag that holds the cash George uses to pay the clammers. These guys are cash and carry, George had told her when she'd argued that writing checks would be better accounting.

"George doesn't like it when you write the combination down." She stands and turns to hand David the money and he is three inches from her, so close that Cassie can tell that he smells sweet, like soap. The safe behind her and the wall to the left block her in. She looks up and finds he's as startled as she is, although it's he who should have given her room. George's voice ends the confusion. "David!" he yells. "What the hell are you doing in there?" At the sound of his father, David takes the cash bag and strides to the door, leaving Cassie and the open safe behind him. He's much taller than his father; everyone knew it was basketball that got him into college, and she can't help but notice how sharp his elbow looks as he lifts the canvas money bag up to signal his father that he's ready to go to work.

Cassie closes the safe because neither George nor old man Cosmo will suffer an open safe.

Although she likes keeping the numbers and papers in order in the office, when she doesn't weigh in the clams Cassie misses the banter with the clam diggers, jokes about rocks or sand clams in the sacks. She finds pleasure in handing out money to people who've earned it, as well as in the authority that comes from recording in the ledger the numbers of pounds taken in. The numbers in the blue ledger are the basis of half the profits. Scallops are the other half, but the scallops came in off the boats, in large and predictable amounts.

As she stands up, she sees the blue ledger left on top of the safe. Cassie grabs it, makes sure a pen is clipped inside, and steps away from the office to find old man Cosmo jogging toward her. She hands him the book. He checks for the pen. "You're a good girl," he says.

"I'm an organized girl," she replies and, all distractions gone, she sits down to the weekly billing. To almost every bill she sends, Cassie can attach a voice, or a story. The Clam Shack in Ipswich, one of their biggest customers, will only take clams a day or two old. The Boat House in the more touristed next town over is less fussy, and so they get Monday morning clams, which have sat since Saturday afternoon and lots of scallops. The Lighthouse in Salem would take lobsters if Cosmo Shellfish had them and, if George or Cosmo were willing, there were the small restaurants in Boston, looking for the fresher North Shore clams, or lobsters, or even mussels. But George and Cosmo aren't willing. They take their profits and buy office buildings and two-family homes and can't understand how Cassie could find fault with a steady, simple income dug from sand.

Cassie types the last of the bills and puts them into envelopes. Maybe David will be different, she thinks. Maybe he'll take after his grandfather, Nicolas. Fresh from Greece, lodging with cousins, the brothers needed to earn a living and Nick chose clams, which were plentiful in Ipswich. Any small outboard could take you to the flats, and after that you needed only a fork, a bag, and a strong back. Nick found the boat, the fork, and the bag, and both brothers knew how to work. That they'd learned on the plains of Sparta. In America only a few months, Nick knew to stay away from the fishing, all done out of Gloucester by the Italian and Portuguese families, and it was Nick who'd ventured to New Bedford to meet the scallop boats coming out of George's Bank. On the rough wall of the office, one of old man Cosmo's daughters has hung a black-and-white photo. The young brothers stand in front of the new Quonset hut, Nick taller and more wiry than his squat brother. Both squint into the sun, fingers curled into their palms, thick from hard work. Fitted into the frame over their heads is a dollar bill, covered in faded Greek script. They look Cassie's age, and Nick is thick-haired and handsome, like his grandson.

When David returns an hour or so later with the ledger and the canvas bag, he heads to the safe and stands in front of it. Cassie wants to ask him what the take was and if Donny, who's been missing for a week and whom she fears was on a bender, showed and whether Freddo's mother has recovered from her fall. Instead, the billing done, she heads out the door, hesitating long enough to see David bend down in front of the safe. Out of the corner of her eye, she sees his graceful fingers move rapidly through the combination and open the safe door, the numbers remembered after all.

The late May sun, sparkling and white, has heated the exterior metal walls of the Quonset hut and Cassie's bike is warm, but she remains chilled inside from the refrigeration, and her eyes can barely open in the bright sunshine. Once she's able to see, she takes Mark's letter from out of her pocket and once again examines the small, block letters that form her name on the thin envelope, Cassandra Leahy. Why does he always write Cassandra on the envelope and Cassie on the letter? That he calls her two names, that he exists at all, somewhere far away, that she's standing here in front of a shiny Quonset hut and can smell the ocean, all of these points seem to her part of a mystery. And this same mystery contains the wet spring wind, the piercing sunshine, and the dirt, so alive beneath her feet that Cassie can sense it pulsing below the gravel parking lot.

Cassie stands, letter in hand and closes her eyes. Spared, Mark is coming home in one piece.

She puts the envelope back in her pocket, climbs onto the bike, and pedals a few wide circles around the lot. As she leans to the side to curve a circle, a loud horn startles her out of her reverie, a blast and then the grate of large tires on gravel. Caught off guard, she lets her wheels slip on the tiny rocks and tip her off the seat onto the ground. Her palms bleed in slits.

"What the fuck Cassie, I nearly fuckin' killed you!" Andy Faragut, a local digger not too much older than Mark, marches toward her, his thin, hard face capped by a dark blue bandana tied tightly over his hair. His arms are taut as he reaches down to pull her up. He's been home from the fighting for almost a year.

"I'm OK."

"Practice for the circus somewhere else next time," he says as he reaches down again to grab her bike.

"Sorry." His eyes are deeply bloodshot. He is stoned most

of the time. There are rumors of heroin.

"Thanks," she adds as she takes the handlebars. And, maybe because she thought she saw a flicker of compassion in his eyes as he handed her the bike, she says, "Mark's coming home. I just heard."

"Yeah, well." Cassie waits for a smile, congratulations, questions, something, but he turns away.

A woman's voice sails from the cab of his truck. "Come on baby!"

"Wait a fucking minute!" Andy yells back. He turns his bloodshot eyes back to Cassie, and there is a glimmer of something in there, maybe sympathy, or maybe more like the twinge you get on your face when someone's elbowed you in the back. "You tell him to look me up when he gets back."

"Sure," she says, but she can't imagine what Mark and Andy would have in common. Andy was all right, but he was so hard all the time. She glances at the truck. The woman, a blond with stringy hair, leans out of the driver's window. She looks familiar, but Andy doesn't bother with introductions. He turns away and heads back to the driver's seat while the blonde woman scrambles back to her side of the cab. He then peels off toward the loading area, late as usual. The old man and George weighed him in late all the time, but they complained afterwards, about having to reopen the safe and sometimes rewash the dock.

Cassie, palms still stinging and feeling foolish, pedals slowly onto the road. She turns back toward town, to retrace her steps toward White's Esso where Stu Camineau, Mark's best friend from before he was shipped away, works.

White's rests across the street from the lines of gray stones that climb the hill in the old cemetery. As she pedals into the station, the radio plays Janis Joplin from inside the little office with dirty windows, "Take a little piece of my heart now, baby." Cassie listens to the ragged, familiar tones. A heart the way Janis sings it isn't any red paper on lace, it's bloody muscle sitting in a pool of blood, so whole, so compact, that there's no way to rip off a section, even gently or neatly, like she just dared someone to reach right into her chest and pull out the whole mass. The guitars end in a solid thump, but the raw spot carved out by the singing hovers in the dusty air.

Stu Camineau is bent over the windshield of a small red Ford. He's got on his mechanic's tan jumpsuit, but his broad shoulders are out of proportion to the rest of his body, so like everything else he wears, the stiff material hangs off him like a tent. As the Ford drives off, he takes the rag tied to his belt loop and cleans each finger, head down and oblivious to the traffic behind him.

"What, did they demote you?" Cassie asks, since she hasn't seen Stu pumping gas in a while, not since he'd fixed a cranky timing belt on his own that Mr. White had left over a weekend.

Stu finishes cleaning his hands. "What, d'you bust the bike again so I have to fix it?"

That comment should make her smile, but Mark's letter has thrown her off. "I got a letter from Mark." She pulls it from her back pocket. "They're sending him home this Thursday."

He looks up, and red blotches pop on his face. "It's early, what's wrong, Cass, what's wrong with Mark?"

"Nothing," she answers quickly. "Why would anything be wrong?" Cassie remembers a letter Mark wrote a couple of months ago about some guy with only a few weeks left in his tour who had some kind of dream about snakes, snakes doubling and tripling themselves around his legs. He was spooked and shot himself in the foot, or maybe the leg, or maybe he shot someone else instead. Mark writes her so many awful stories that they all blend into one.

"That's how it's done, Stu. They just pull him out of patrol one day and ship him home the next."

"Holy shit."

Cassie looks up at the sky. The clouds are the puffy white

spring clouds that sheep jump over in baby books. Stu hadn't been drafted.

"Is he all right with that?"

"I don't know," she admits. "He didn't say." She unfolds the letter.

"I'm not reading your mail," he says and holds his hands up.

He looks so funny, red-faced and terrified, that she laughs and waves the letter at him. "It's not a hand grenade," she teases.

"That's not funny." He takes a step back. "It's none of my business."

Mr. White, a trim, thin man with a precise mustache, pulls open the office door. "Stu," he shouts over a mad guitar riff on the radio, "time to lift the block back in!" He turns back again, "And stop changing the station every time I turn my goddamn back!"

"Gotta go, Cass. You going out tonight?"

She replaces the letter in her back pocket. "I'm meeting Teri Pinter at the Pub."

He looks serious at the mention of her name, but Teri did that to people. In a town where few of the students went on to four-year colleges and most everyone settled within five miles of their parents' house, Teri Pinter was different. "OK, then. Thanks for coming by, Cass."

He's so careful with her, gentle almost, that Cassie resists the urge to bury her face in his jumpsuit. He would think she was cracking up, or worse, get the wrong idea. "Hey Stu," she says. "If you go out, be sure to come on over and say hello to Teri."

He nods and heads toward the bays.

Cassie gets back on her bike. She remembers a late night at the beach, the sand still warm from the day's sun and the moon so bright the dunes glowed a thousand shades of blue. "Look," she'd said as she'd rolled onto her side, "how warm the sand still is over here." "I'm not going," Mark had said to her. "I just won't go." She'd rolled back to him, the sand gritty between their skin, caught in the strands of their hair, and there was no one else. Not a light, not a shout, not an airplane overhead, just the lap of the waves on the wet shore and the blue dunes under the moon.

His day off, Frank Leahy is fifteen feet from where his daughter left him this morning. Dressed now, with the drapes pulled so that the sun doesn't shine on the screen, he's moved to the couch to watch the Red Sox game on TV.

Cassie sits down next to him. She can tell from the back-stop that the game's not at Fenway and from the pitcher's uniform that they're playing Detroit. The season's barely a month old, and most of the players are wearing their long sleeve jerseys in the wet Michigan weather. "How long has it been raining?"

"A couple of innings, but we're into the eighth, so they could call it anytime now. I got us a nice piece of fish for dinner. You hungry? I'm going to batter it up, make some cole slaw."

"Sounds good, Dad." In the darkened room Cassie, sleepy, leans back against the couch. Mark used to watch the game with her dad. She wonders if he'll still want to. Two batters reach base before her father speaks again.

"You going out tonight?"

"I'm meeting Teri Pinter down at the Pub." She yawns. "But not 'til later."

"Damn." The batter on the screen throws his bat to the ground. "He's swinging at anything within five miles of the plate."

When her dad's done fixing it, the fish is fresh and white on the inside, with a light batter on the outside, and the slaw is more vinegary than mayonnaise, the way Cassie likes it.

"Where did you get the fish?" she asks because it tastes perfect, as if it flopped off a boat this afternoon.

"Teddy ran it by, on his way in."

Cassie nods. Her father, widowed for years now, cannot accurately relate his intricate network of friends and acquaintances. Teddy, if it's the right Teddy, works at the firehouse and has a small boat. But most of them have some kind of boat, and people are always bringing things by. Or else her father's slipped out to drop something else off. Who could keep track? Cassie gets up to clear the dishes.

"Can you put a few pieces on a plate?" he asks.

She nods and reaches for a dish that wasn't one of her mother's. Even though most of them do return eventually, it could be months before this one threads its way back. After arranging a generous serving of fish and cole slaw, Cassie leaves the plate covered in plastic wrap on the counter. She has long stopped asking him who the plates were for. Frank will take it somewhere on his way out, just as freshly caught fish, garden tomatoes, cookies, and flowers will find their way back. Sometimes though, maybe when they're out grabbing a bite at the roast beef shop, an anonymous donor or recipient will appear. An older lady in black, say, or a man she's never seen before, will stop and pat her father on the back and smile at Cassie. "And this is your daughter," they'll say. "You must be very proud."

"Who's that?" she'll ask after they've moved on. "That's old Johnny McGuire," is all Frank will say, as if that fully answered all her questions.

Frank Leahy is showered and out the door before his daughter is ready to leave. Most likely he'll go down to the K Club or, despite the fact he never made it farther than Virginia during the last war and was safely home and married by the time Korea came around, to the VFW for a few drinks and some company. Cassie doesn't ask and he doesn't volunteer. Still, she always tells him where she's going to be, an old habit neither of them are ready to break.

The sunlight's gone by seven thirty, but in the Pub it's always dark. Still a bit early for the drinking crowd, at the bar sit the usual middle-aged men working on their dinners. One, in a white T-shirt, gray hair parted neatly and black shoes shined, is working on roast chicken with the concentration he might have in his own kitchen, the TV blaring behind him.

Cassie finds Teri on a stool at a small table behind the bar. She looks relieved when Cassie comes around her and taps her on the shoulder.

"Hey, Cassie!" Teri glances over her shoulder. "I've never been in here before. I had no idea it was so popular."

Cassie shrugs. "There's no where else to go."

"Cassie. Anyone in here could drive for twenty minutes and find somewhere else to go. In an hour, we could all be in Boston."

"That's not what I meant."

"You just sounded like such a townie."

"So?" she says, but smiles. "See my boyfriend over there?" She points to the middle-aged man in the white T-shirt. "I'm going to have his baby. Do you want to be in my wedding? It's gonna have to be quick, though, before I show too much." Cassie sips her beer.

"You're disgusting." Teri always laughs at her jokes. Lately it seems to Cassie that she goes weeks before she's around someone who makes her want to joke.

"But Teri, the one to his right's his brother. You could have him. We could live next door to each other and have too many children and let ourselves go."

"And I could practice out of the tool shed."

"Practice?"

"Yeah, I'm applying to med school."

"Doctor Teri," Cassie says quietly.

"I need to take the right courses, do the right thing during the summer, plan ahead. There's not as many spots for women, you know, so it's harder to get in."

"Huh."

"I don't know for sure, but my advisor says it's true. They want to save more spots for people who actually have to earn a living."

Cassie snorts.

"Yeah, well, I'm not going to change the," she lowers her voice, "system."

Out of the corner of her eye, Cassie sees Stu lurking at the bar, and she shifts her gaze so he can't catch her eye. "Are you gonna do that same science thing this summer?"

"No," Teri hesitates. "Cassie, there's some guy over there, next to the father of your child, who keeps staring over here. Do you know him?"

"I'm sure I don't," says Cassie.

"He's waving," says Teri. "Now he's coming over here."

Stu plunks down a bottle on their table. His hair flips in little curls around his chin as if he'd just come out of the shower and it hasn't completely dried. He looks a lot sharper that he usually does, but his clothes still hang. "Hi Cassie! How are you doing Teri? Long time, no see!"

"Stu," says Cassie for Teri's benefit. "Have you seen Teri since we all graduated?"

"No, I don't think I have. Not since you gave that great speech at graduation, Teri."

Cassie doubts Stu could remember a word of Teri's speech, or even listened to a word of it while she gave it, but if she confronted him with these facts, he'd be confused, even hurt. Sure Teri gave a good speech! Sure he enjoyed it!

It's clearly Teri's turn to say something, but she's stuck on the fact she has no idea who Stu is. Cassie sends a silent message to Teri: You were in the same class for six years, say something! This seems to work. Teri speaks. "Hi, ah, Stu, it's good to see you too!"

Pitifully little to go on, but Stu's not fussy. "So what are you up to this summer, Teri?"

Teri maintains a formal smile. "Well, ah, Stu, this summer I'll be on the Pine Ridge Indian Reservation as a medical assistant."

"Wow," says Stu.

Cassie's eyes sting and water at this new information.

Stu notices first. "You all right, Cassie?"

"Something in my eye, I'll be OK," she answers into a cocktail napkin.

"It's a program to bring medical attention to poorly served areas," Teri continues. "And premed students are selected from a pool of applicants to serve for a summer."

"That's something," says Stu. "So you're not getting paid for this either?"

"No, it's strictly volunteer. The community can't afford to pay us."

"Cassie, you sure you're all right?" Cassie nods. She can't explain herself the overwhelming sadness that came to her when Teri said she wouldn't spend the summer in Ipswich. But what had Cassie expected? Teri can't stay here.

"Maybe you should have Doctor Teri take a look at you." Stu laughs.

Cassie looks up. "It's out now."

"That's good," says Teri.

"Cassie, did you tell your friend Teri your big news?"

Cassie glares at Stu.

"What news, Cassie?"

She wants to say no news, but one look at Stu and she can't. It is her big news, and she can't help it that it's not really even about her. "Mark's coming home in a few weeks."

Teri puts on her formal smile again. "Well, I'm glad he's OK."

"It'll be great to see him," says Stu.

"I didn't know you were still that close, after he left to, you know."

Teri's words hang, charged, but then the jukebox switches on, and someone yells for Stu.

He grabs his beer. "Gotta go."

"He was drafted, you know that, he didn't choose to go," points out Cassie, although she knows that story doesn't work for Teri. In Teri's world, everyone always has a choice. "We wrote back and forth," she adds into the silence.

"Were you waiting for him?" asks Teri. She'd be good as a surgeon, thinks Cassie. She could just cut out what she didn't like.

"Nothing was that formal," answers Cassie. "So," she shifts uneasily under her friend's microscope. "Tell me about the Indians."

Later that night, Cassie stands in the yellow kitchen, with just the small light on over the sink. The windows are closed, but the room is crisp with spring chill and Cassie shivers as she takes Mark's letter from her back pocket and opens it up. "Dear Cassie," she reads. "They're finally sending me home. Which is a good thing, because baby I'm at the end of my rope here. The guys are all gone now. Every goddamn one of them and there's no one left, just like I told you. And Cass you don't owe me anything. I want you to know that. Love, Mark." She puts the letter on the counter.

Through the letters, in a way they are closer now than they were when he left. She remembers the first thing he wrote that made her think, he would never tell me this. It was about being afraid, so scared that his insides felt all loose and gone, like goo. How do you look into the face of someone who's told you that? Something about writing the words down must make it easier to say them. It certainly makes it easier to listen.

When Cassie was little, she used to be able to close her eyes, just before she dropped off to sleep and imagine, really feel, her mother's warm arms around her. It was so true that she almost wanted to open her eyes to catch a glimpse, but she never did, never dared to. It has been a while since that trick worked for her.

Cassie folds the letter back into her pocket. Maybe she and Mark would just pick up from where they'd left off, but that's never the way it works. The days move forward like the swift current at changing tide. You can try as hard as you can to swim or stand in place, but the water's always rushing past you, carrying fish and seaweed and whatever else is caught up in its pull, reminding you how hard it is to stand still and that, sooner or later, the effort will exhaust you, and you will have no choice but to let go.

**June 4, 1971**

Unseasonably warm, no breeze blows through the wide-open windows, and the small house is an oven.

Cassie, wet from her shower, searches rapidly in the back of her bureau for some summer clothes. Mark's family is due to pick her up in a matter of minutes to join them in the trip to the airport to greet Mark as he returns home.

She pulls out clothes according to touch. Her good jeans roll out first, but they're heavy and thick in the heat, so she reaches deeper into her dresser. As Cassie shifts the unfolded mass forward, her hand touches something soft and silky. She tugs. Her team shorts, bright red, part of her track uniform from high school, slip smoothly out.

Cassie steps back to sit on her bed. She was supposed to return the shorts to the school with the rest of the uniform, but she'd kept them, to practice in. With a strict personal training regimen during high school that included running through the off-season and weight training with cans of stewed tomatoes on the weekends, in her mind, she'd earned them.

Cassie brings the soft material to her face. The shorts are cool and light.

It's been three years since she ran her personal best time in the eight-eighty, two times around the track, to send her to the states for the second year in a row, three years from the day she met Mark.

When Cassie thinks about that day and the meet, she remembers how hundreds of bright yellow buttercups sat low to the grass along the gravel. Last-minute stretches, a luxury of warm muscle, and the gunshot rang out. Her sneakers hit the track and then there was the sense of pulling and being pulled along that running brings, as her elbows and legs powered out in a perfect beat. She sped along the oval like that for the whole race, her teammates' cheers in the background, the other runners a distance behind.

At the finish line, she felt she'd been given a gift, and no one had to tell her she'd just run the fastest race of her life. Cassie knelt in the buttercups as her teammates crowded around, and they'd mistaken her supplication for exhaustion.

She wonders if she hadn't won that race that afternoon so spectacularly whether she would have later met Mark as she did, head on, without fear and with complete confidence in her ability to navigate any situation.

"Watch for my ride, for my friend Mark," Stu told her after the meet as she sat on the front steps of the high school. "He drives an old car." When a green Chevy pulled in from the street and cruised down the long driveway, she knew the car would stop for her, just as she knew the late afternoon sun would dip behind the school at the same instant she stood up, just as she knew she'd win her race.

As she walked down the school steps to his car, she felt beautiful in her old green sweatshirt and silky track shorts, her legs muscled and her cheeks still flushed from the race. When she grabbed the sides of the car through the open window and looked in, Mark was in the driver's seat. He was compact, with broad shoulders, hair that hung straight, and the darkest brown eyes she'd ever seen.

She hasn't gone running in almost a year, never wore the shorts after her last track meet in high school. Cassie rolls the shorts back up into a ball and throws them into the drawer.

Maybe at a four-year college she could have run track

again, but she hadn't bothered to find that out before she'd graduated high school. Some of the boys had gotten calls from college track coaches, but no one had called the girls. She remembers Teri's lowered voice at the Pub, whispering "the system" when she'd acknowledged that there were fewer slots for girls in medical school. Well, maybe so, but it was no one's fault but her own that she hadn't applied to a four-year college her senior year, that she'd enrolled at the local community college instead, and that she hadn't kept up running her miles.

A car horn bursts four or five times. No time left for anything but the jeans. She pulls them on, races outside and up the side of the house as Mark's brother, Pete, pulls into the driveway.

Paul, Mark's eight-year-old nephew, hangs his head out of the back window and hollers, "We're late!"

"Paul! Paul! Get your head back in the car this instant," shouts his mother, Ann.

Cassie opens the back door and glances at the hot, nervous passengers. Mark's father, Ed, and Pete are in the front seat. Mark's mother, Peg, Ann, and three red-faced children are packed in the back. She hesitates.

"Kids!" barks Ann. "Get in the back! Now! Move out!" The occupants spring into action. Four-year-old Lisa leaps with glee over the back seat into the vast, padded way-back of the wagon. Paul rolls his eyes and slings himself after his sister. The baby, released from the bookends of her siblings, slips on her sweaty thighs along the plastic seat onto the floor and wails.

"Open the back! Open the back door Dad! Please!" chants Paul over his baby sister's howls.

Lisa joins in. "Open the back! Open the back!" they sing.

"Stop the yelling!" shouts Ann.

Peg Harris bends down to scoop up her granddaughter. She smoothes the baby's plastered hair and damp face. "Shush,

shush," she croons. "Uncle Mark doesn't want to come home and find you all upset."

Ed Harris smiles at Cassie from the safety of the front seat. "There's plenty of room." He pats the ten inches that separate him from his son in the driver's seat. "I'll just slide over to the door a bit more."

"She doesn't want to squeeze in," admonishes Peg. "Come on back here, Cassie. It'll be just fine when we get started and get a breeze going. The kids'll stay in back, won't you?" She turns and smiles at her grandchildren.

"Yes Grandma!" they chorus back.

The motorcycle that pulls into the driveway stops all conversation. The children peer out the back window as Stu turns the motor off and knocks the kickstand down. He's wearing a denim jacket with the arms cut out that Cassie's never seen before and jeans that slide down over his hips; his hair dangles scraggly over his shoulders. "Oh, Ed," Peg says. She reaches her spare hand to her husband's shoulder. "It's Stu. I'm so glad he's here."

The station wagon makes Stu shy and, as he ducks his head down to speak to Mark's family, Cassie notices that in the heat some of his curls have stuck to the skin on his neck.

"I want to go on the motorcycle!" Paul calls out.

"Me too!" echoes Lisa.

Ann cuts in. "No one is going on the motorcycle."

Stu smiles at the children, as if he doesn't notice that their bright red, overheated faces, their high-pitched squealing, and their incessant jumping in the way-back is any different from the adult behavior in the front seats. "You need to listen to your mother," he tells them gently, and they beam back at him. "I just thought I'd follow you to the airport," he says to Peg.

"Why, sure," says Peg. "That would be wonderful."

"Mom, we got to get going," says Pete.

"Cassie," Stu says, in a low voice. "They got room for you

in there?”

"We've got room for an army in here," answers Peg. "Don't we?”

"We make as much noise as an army," says Ann.

"You can ride with me," Stu offers.

Ed pats the seat between him and Pete. "Once we get going, it won't be so hot in here! We'll get some air!”

Cassie leans into the back seat. "I'll go with Stu," she says.

Paul and Lisa protest. "We want Cassie! We want Cassie!”

"You sure you want to ride all the way to Boston on that …," Ann hesitates, "bike?”

Cassie shrugs and slides onto the back of the seat after Stu. "Remember not to look down," he says before he starts the engine. Cassie pokes him in the back as she rests two hands on his waist. She remembers the time they drove down the beach road and the sight of the gravel whipping under her feet had made her dizzy. That feels like a long time ago now.

Mark's homecoming is so big that Cassie can't even think about it. Instead, it's the nerves she feels, the jittery, shallow way she's been breathing all morning, the way her hands shake and can't be still. She worries that she hasn't had a letter since the one announcing his homecoming despite that, in a usual week, she'd have received two more by now. But, she tells herself, he must have been too busy to write.

The trees zip by, making her head spin, so she watches Stu's back. The moving bike forces a breeze, mostly warm, with patches of cool that feel as if they came in from over the water, and the sweaty, overheated feeling Cassie had all morning is almost gone. Paul and Lisa, their faces on the lookout from the back of the station wagon, make her smile.

On Route 1 the air is hot and gassy. Cassie scoots closer to Stu's wide back in the increasing traffic. The children lean their red faces against the sides of the window, staring out.

At one red light, Stu calls back. "Has Teri Pinter gone to

the Indians?"

"What?"

"What the hell is she thinking? Shit," he adds as the light turns green, "she didn't even know who I was."

Cassie waits impatiently for the next red light, but Stu speaks first. "She could have stayed here. Some of those babies down Millet Road could use a doctor."

Cassie wants to set him straight. She should let him know that Teri's never coming back home, that she's talked about leaving Ipswich since the seventh grade. "She'll recognize you the next time she sees you," she says.

"You know, that's right, Cassie. I hadn't thought of that." He cuts between a long snake of traffic, to the head of the line waiting for the light.

Cassie is tempted to knock her forehead against his back like you might knock your head against a brick wall, but the scenery distracts her. The deep-water port, the tankers, and the gas tanks zip along on the right, and soon they are on the curving ramp to the airport.

The vast asphalt parking lot glares and shimmers in the heat. Cassie stumbles off the bike. Stu reaches out and catches her elbow.

Pete, purple in the face and hair matted to his head with sweat, pulls up next to them. "The plane's due in now. Go on in and we'll catch up."

Stu pulls at Cassie's arm. "Let's go," he urges.

Inside the terminal, Cassie shivers in the sterile cold. It's as chilly in the terminal as in the Cosmo fish locker. "Come on," Stu says. "We need to find the gate." A crisp blond woman behind the counter tells them that the plane from San Francisco is coming in at Gate 12. Stu takes off, with Cassie following behind.

They race past a ladies' room. In the cooler air and with the passengers mostly dressed for traveling, Cassie is conscious of the dirt and dried sweat from the ride on her face and neck. "Wait!" she calls without stopping for an answer and ducks inside. At the sink, she runs warm water over her chilled hands and splashes her face and neck. The warmth gives her goose bumps, and she's aware of her heart beating quicker than feels comfortable. In the mirror, her eyes look large and red. She splashes more water on her face and then dries herself off with harsh brown paper towels, aware that time is passing and that the plane could be in. She knows, though, that Stu will wait for her.

He does. He grabs her arm again, and they sprint down the wide corridor, weaving in and out of the crowds, both understanding that they'll need to pass the lady with the heavy bag on the left six feet before they get to her, but the man in the brown suit they can pass just at the last moment and on the right. The running exhilarates Cassie and when she reaches the gate, she fidgets from foot to foot to keep the comfort of motion.

The gate is crowded. One man, angular, gawky, jeans slipping halfway down his narrow hips, jumps toward them.

"Did Larry send you down? Where are the signs?" His beady blue eyes assume an answer.

"We're here to meet someone," answers Cassie.

"I'm Dennis. Are you here to meet Dennis?"

"No," says Stu, his voice louder than necessary.

The gawky man holds his hand in the air and makes a 'V' sign as he backs away toward a group of young people dressed in jeans. "It's cool. That's cool."

Cassie, embarrassed, turns away. The group of kids are probably students, she thinks, students at four-year schools.

"I have a bad feeling about that guy," says Stu.

"Cassie! Cassie!" Paul and Lisa race straight toward her, barely skirting the adults in their way. They stop short and look shyly up at Stu. "Is Uncle Mark here yet?" asks Paul.

"Is he here yet?" echoes his sister, who is too young to remember when her Uncle Mark left home.

"Not yet," says Stu, "but if you look out the window, maybe you can see his plane coming in."

A plane pulls up on the tarmac. The crowd pulls tight together, and Cassie loses sight of the children.

"Paul! Lisa!" Ann and Pete, red-faced baby in her father's arms, make their way through the busy corridor, with Peg and Ed a few feet behind, arm-in-arm and tight, expectant looks that tilt both their faces up.

Cassie grabs for Stu's hand, catches herself, and hugs herself across the chest. Stu glances down at her, and she gives a mock shiver. "It's cold in here," she says. "Like a fish locker."

Ann and Peg gather the older children.

The gawky man with the loose jeans leaps into the stream of passengers filing off the plane. What he holds at arms' length is hidden by the swarm of people. His small gang begins to chant. "Mai Lai! Mai Lai!"

"What the hell are they saying?" Pete explodes and shifts the baby from the crook of one elbow to the other.

Ed crosses his arms, sets back onto his heels. "It doesn't make any difference what they say."

Lisa spots Mark first, easily identifies him as the only person visible in uniform. "Uncle Mark! Uncle Mark!" she shouts and runs, arms outstretched.

Cassie looks up for Mark and sees a uniform, stiff and dull green, shiny black shoes, and the hat that covers his face. The buttons glint, and her eyes rest on his hands, the only part of him that looks familiar.

Lisa is nearly to Mark, when the gawky man steps between them. He lifts a yellow bucket and throws something red, like blood. Mark's chest is splattered with it; it runs on the floor at his feet. The man then turns toward the crowd and holds the bucket high in the air, like a sword.

Everyone moves at once.

Paul screams, "He's been shot! He's been shot!" Pete tries to pass the baby off to Ann, but she's bent over to receive the retreating Lisa. Stu lunges forward, but Mark grabs Stu behind the arms with a quick, compact movement that holds him. The man and the bucket disappear.

"It's just tomato juice," Mark says. "What you put on dogs when they run into a skunk." Whatever expression Cassie expects to see on Mark's face at this moment, it isn't the one she sees, briefly, before he hides it under a sort of smile. Mark looks as if someone has just hit him on the side of the head and he has all he can do to hold the pain of the blow inside. He drops Stu's arms. Stu takes a few quick steps, but the gawky man and his friends have disappeared into the crowd.

Into the silence that follows, Peg steps up and holds Mark in quick, tight, hug. The other Harris's follow, save Lisa, who can't be convinced that Mark's not covered in blood.

They stand in an awkward circle. "Cassie came too," says Ed, as he steps back to reveal Cassie hovering at the outskirts.

He looks over her head now and pulls her to a hug. He has to. The whole family stands around them with their mouths hanging open a bit for extra oxygen, watching the reunited lovers.

The uniform is scratchy and stiff, the hat bumps against her face, and his body is hard and unyielding. All that remains of Mark is a soft part of his neck as it brushes up against her cheek. A faint scent of his sweat, a small patch of heat: Cassie closes her eyes to capture this, and he pulls away. She opens them again.

"Well," says Ed. "Let's get this show on the road."

"Geezus," Stu mutters to Cassie as they move back down the corridor. "Why the hell did he just take it like that?"

Cassie watches Mark's back as he leads the parade back. His hands, hanging tight and curled by his side, do not invite her to grab hold of them, to lock their fingers together to swing playfully between them. The front of her shirt has a red blotch from the tomato juice. Peg's white blouse has a spoiled front, as does Ed's, Pete's, Ann's, and Paul's, everyone but Stu and Lisa. But no one mentions the stains. Instead, Pete comments on the unseasonably hot weather, and Peg notes that Mark hasn't much baggage after being away for so long.

In the parking lot, overhead jets take off and land in a noisy stream. Exhaust and gasoline hang in the warm air, and the faces of the Harris family have taken on an oily, sweaty sheen. Pete opens the back of the wagon for Mark's duffel bag, and the children pile in after. "We can use it like a big pillow," Lisa tells her brother.

"Why don't you sit in the front," Ed says to his son.

Lisa leans out the back and looks at Cassie. "Come back here," she coaxes, "and ride home on the big pillow."

Paul pushes his sister. "I want to ride home on the motorcycle!"

"You'll do no such thing!" retorts Ann.

"What motorcycle?" asks Mark. They all turn to him because it's the first thing he's said since they left the terminal.

"Mine." And when Mark looks confused, Stu says, "The same one. It's parked on the other side of the car."

All eyes follow Mark as he walks over to the bike. "You painted it," he remarks.

Now all eyes are turned to Stu because it's clear that Mark would rather go home alone on the motorcycle than in the crowded car, hot and full of his family. Even the children stay still in the back of the wagon as they watch their uncle and Stu. They all want to please Mark, but no one would blame Stu, either, if he wanted to ride his own bike home. Cassie looks down at her feet. Of course Stu will give him the bike. Stu would walk home if he had to.

"Take the bike home yourself." He hands over the keys.

Mark nods and moves to the back of the car. The kids scramble out of the way as he strips down to his skin, his back a waxy green color despite a tan. He's so thin the nubs of his spine pop up as he bends over his duffel and pulls out a gray T-shirt. Cassie wants to reach out and rub her palms down the bones, wants him to turn around and kiss her, hold her. If only his family wasn't here, then he'd be different. He'd be able to look at her and tell her how much he's missed her. They could be alone together again.

She puts her hands in her pockets and looks over at Stu. He may have given over his bike, but he's not riding shotgun.

"Stu, you ride in the front with Pete," says Ed.

"No sir, Mr. Harris."

"Well, you'll ride in the back with me," says Peg. "You can't walk home."

"What about Cassie?" asks Ann.

Mr. Harris pats the front seat as he climbs in next to his older son. "There's always room for Cassie right here."

Mark shoves the duffel into the back of the wagon. "Cassie can ride with me," he says.

Mark sits. His shiny dress shoes crease as he rocks the kick-stand back, revs the engine, and glances toward her, with a flat kind of waiting look, to get on the bike.

If only his face held any anticipation of her joining him, she'd feel differently.

There might be some kind of bus home, or she could wait for her father to get home from work. Maybe Teri could borrow her parent's car and come and pick her up, if she weren't out on some last-minute errands getting ready for her summer with the Indians.

"Let's go," he shouts over the engine.

She slips onto the seat and reaches to his waist for support. His hair, though short, is the same straight, deep brown. His back, though harder and thinner, sits between familiar shoulders. She moves to lean her cheek against his shirt, but he takes off, fast, and she pulls backward instead.

Mark doesn't follow his brother. He rides between the lanes, passes the cars stuck in the late afternoon traffic, and at times speeds up through intersections as the lights flip from yellow to red. At some yellows he skids short, and the heated tires smell of burnt rubber. He wants me here, Cassie tells herself, even though he makes no effort to say hello at the red lights or to reach back to see how she's doing. Rather than lean back against her, his back stays straight.

The seat on Stu's bike is flat, not a little raised at the rear like some, so unless she makes an effort, her only view is of Mark's back. Into her second hour on the bike, her arms are tense, and she tries hard not to look down as the asphalt zips below her.

In this way, they make their way back home. As they move through the woods just before town, Mark abruptly pulls to the side of the road and stops the bike. He dismounts and walks into the woods, out of sight. A wayward seagull squawks overhead; Cassie arches her neck back. The unseasonable heat of the day disappears as the sun moves below the treetops, and the chilly shadows creep across the road toward the brush. Most likely Mark has to pee, but for all Cassie knows he just decided to walk the rest of the way on his own.

Mark appears suddenly at her side. He takes her hand, puts something in it, and closes her fingers around it into a fist.

"What?" she begins, but he shakes his head at her as if to say, I can't, hops back on the bike, and peels away from the shoulder.

She holds one hand over the other where he touched her. He leaves no time to open her fist to see what he put in there, before she must grip his waist for support as they move out.

In town, they don't take the turn to Mark's house. Then they miss the turn for Cassie's street too. They run through downtown and out again for another mile or two. Maybe he's just taking a tour, she thinks. He hasn't been home in over a year.

He turns into the Clam Shack, parks the bike near a picnic bench, and turns the engine off.

Paul and Lisa's voices grow louder as Pete pulls up behind them. "The Clam Shack! The Clam Shack!" they sing, almost like a song. "We knew you'd be at the Clam Shack!"

Cassie opens her fist. On the palm of her hand sits a small, green leaf. White drops bleed from where stem has been torn from the plant, milkweed.

The Harris family has escaped the car and is making its way toward the order window. "I was hungry," Mark says to his mother. He reaches into his back pocket. "Look, I cashed my check in Hawaii. I can even treat."

Pete, a few steps behind Ann, turns back to his mother and brother. "I can treat my baby brother to a couple buckets," he says and hands Ann his wallet.

Stu, though, is already at the window.

"Sit down Mom and Dad," Ann says as she hands the baby over to Peg. "Let me order for the children!" she shouts at Stu.

The children have found the condiment shelf. Paul opens a ketchup packet and squirts it against his shirt. He throws his arms in the air and shrieks, "You got me!"

Lisa screams. "Do that to me! Do it to me too!"

"OK, then," concedes Mark to Pete and sits down on the picnic bench. Cassie sits down next to Peg. Mark's face is much thinner than she remembers. She wishes she could see his eyes, but with his back to the setting sun, his face is shadowy. He must remember too, she thinks, that afternoon just after they'd first met, when he'd found milkweed in her backyard. Even after all he's been through, he didn't forget that. Now she's sure that when the Harris family goes home, he'll talk to her.

Paul and Lisa run by, each covered in ketchup. All eyes watch as they turn around the benches and head back to the gravel lot.

As Stu and Ann return, Cassie stuffs the leaf into her pocket. "We ordered you some clams," Ann says to her, "if you're not sick of looking at them."

"Cassie loves fried clams," says Mark, loudly, but to himself, as if both Cassie and the fried clams were a million miles away.

Mark looks up at her, and she looks back at the shadowy face, the short straight hair, the arms crossed in front of his chest.

"It's true," she says, "I do. I never get sick of them."

Pete is looking at his shoes, Ed scratches some itch behind his knee, Peg bounces the baby, and Ann gets up to fetch the food.

"Well," she admits. "I might some day."

He nods his head at her.

"But then," she adds, "I might not. I might never get sick of them."

Lisa, front dripping red, races between them, turns back to her brother, and falls in a heap to the ground. Her arms and legs shake and hit the ground and she turns her head toward her baby sister. "Look," she whispers, "Look what Paul did to me."

Mark nods again at Cassie. "OK. That could happen too."

"Oh Lordy," says Peg. "Now look what you've done. Just wait 'til your mother gets hold of you."

Lisa rolls onto her back. "She won't care Gramma," she says. "She won't care because she loves me."

Cassie stares back at Mark as Ann returns with the tray. "That's right," she repeats his words. "That could happen too."


The front of the house is dark. Cassie and Mark walk along the side, toward the back, to where the kitchen light sprays into the night. Frank Leahy sits in the kitchen in his back-less house slippers reading the sports page, open can of beer at his side. He is clean, hair combed down slick, wearing a laundry-fresh undershirt and slacks. Every workday holds the same routine and, once home, Frank Leahy doesn't do anything else until he's showered. Years ago, when he was still on the dyeing floor, his wife had objected to his yellow fingers and to the smell of raw leather that clung to him like a cooking odor. Even though he is a floor manager now, the shower habit stays.

They come in through the back door, into the kitchen. Her father looks up from his paper. The temperature has dropped, but the windows remain open, and the house is cold.

He stands. "Mark! Welcome home! It's good to see you, son." The two men walk toward each other and shake hands awkwardly.

Mark smiles back, tight, as if he were squinting under a thousand bulbs, not the weak overheads of the Leahy kitchen. Cassie rubs her arms in the cold, rolls the kitchen windows shut, and peers into the dark rooms past the doorway.

"No game tonight?" Mark asks.

"They're playing on the west coast."

"They should have a good year."

"Ah," complains Frank. "You'll have to come by and watch me get my heart broken this season."

Mark almost smiles.

Frank nods. Cassie knows her father is not one to fill empty space with words. A single dish sits drying on the rack, next to a stack of pans. "What did you cook?" Cassie asks to break the quiet.

Frank smiles. "Liver and onions."

She sniffs at the sweet, heavy smell of fried onions, mixed with something less appealing. "I guess you weren't expecting me."

"I guess I wasn't." He sips his beer. "But there's leftovers in the fridge." He looks at Mark. "You hungry? Would you like a beer?"

"Pete, and Stu too, took us all to the Clam Shack," answers Cassie.

"Well," says Mark. "Gotta go."

Cassie turns to him. Where are we going, she wants to ask, but he moves toward the door without looking at her and she understands that she's being left behind. A rush of blood makes her throat thick; she wants to grab his arm, keep him here, or follow him out the door, but she can't, not with her father watching.

He waves an arm at them and slips out the back door. Cassie fights herself not to run after him. Her father sits back down at the table, his beer untouched at his side.

Cassie remembers going to Teri Pinter's house after school. Mrs. Pinter, who wore a different pretty headband every day, always asked them how school went. Even into junior and high school, Mrs. Pinter asked, every afternoon, how was the day? Her own dad never asked. But when they sat down to eat, somehow the information slipped out, even during the times when she'd sworn that she wouldn't tell him a thing.

Now, she can't find any words. With her dad watching, she rubs her palms over her eyes to prevent their tearing, taking some slow deep breaths. In the silence of the kitchen, she can picture the tears and the noise and the crashing about that would come with her letting the first word of complaint out. The commotion would then fade away and she knows she'd be left, after the scene, in the same place she is now only more tired. She may as well skip the messy part.

She had been wrong to think that it was the Harris's that stopped Mark from talking to her. It was more than that—he wasn't himself.

Her shoulders hunch up. "Gees, Dad, it's freezing in here."

"Well. The house was hotter than hell when I got home."

"I gotta close some windows."

"Teri called for you. An hour or so ago."

"But she's in South Dakota. With her Indians." This last part slips out like a whine.

"She's says she's home."

"They leave, they come home. It's like a revolving door around here." Cassie walks toward the living room.

"Cassie. It's gonna take a while before he knows his ass from his elbow."

"Who made you so smart?"

"Maybe I never got shipped overseas, but I've seen it. All those guys who were a little older than me. Look at Spooky Wilson."

Cassie turns back, angry. "Are you saying Mark is Spooky Wilson?"

"I'm just saying Spooky wasn't always like he is now. He went to Europe one way and came home another."

"Mark is not Spooky Wilson. Right Dad?"

"Mark is not Spooky Wilson." He looks out at the darkened window, and Cassie follows his gaze, but there's nothing out there. Even if there were, they couldn't see it beyond the glare of the kitchen lights.

"I just don't want you to be Mrs. Spooky Wilson, that's all," and he laughs at his own joke. He turns his head toward Cassie to check if she's still angry. But Cassie laughs too, because she as Mrs. Spooky Wilson is a ridiculous thought. For one thing, Spooky Wilson is way too old for her and for another, since he doesn't say too much, no one even knows what's in his head, if anything. As if someone like Mark could ever end up like that.

But tonight he wasn't himself. Or maybe his new self is no longer interested in her. Maybe when he'd written her that she didn't owe him anything, what he'd meant was that he felt he didn't owe her anything.

Cassie's so cold now she can feel the chilled tips of her fingers through her sweatshirt. She shivers.

"Give it time," says her father.

Cassie nods. She heads to the living room to close the windows.

## June 5, 1971

Cassie raises her right palm and pushes against Cosmo Shellfish's front door. But the door stays closed and a jab of blocked force runs backward and rests at her shoulder.

"Ow," she says. She reaches for the knob, but it doesn't turn. Cassie leans into the door, shoves her side against it once, then twice, but it doesn't budge. That the door is locked takes a few minutes to sink in. The door is never locked. Never, in almost four years, has Cassie showed up for work before either old man Cosmo or George.

She leans her back against the door and rubs her arms in the early morning chill. A cool fog has replaced yesterday's stifling heat, and droplets like crystal adhere to the gravel, to her hair, to the wires strung between the telephone poles. It can't be much past six and, there's no one else in sight.

A small black bird with a few shiny green feathers on his chest flits back and forth in the upper branches of a freshly budded maple tree near the sidewalk. Its constant motion and twittering remind Cassie of all there is to do this morning, the delivery trucks need to go out, the shuckers are due in shortly, and there's also an early low tide.

She turns back to the doorknob, a simple brass one not unlike the front door of her house and gives it another futile turn. Worn to dull and a little loose in its sockets, it doesn't seem fair that this old lock is all that stands between her and entry. At this thought, Cassie reaches into her front pocket for a key that dangles on a silver loop, the key to her house. She has carried this key on its silver loop since grade school, even though her father has never locked the kitchen door, ever since she found it in the pocket of her mother's navy blue sweater that hung in her father's closet for years, until Mrs. Hooper came and cleared all the clothes away. Ghosts, she'd called them, and her father hadn't protested. But when the clothes were gone, what was left was the empty half of a closet, and Cassie found she preferred the ghosts, the wayward brush of a well-worn cardigan, to what was left, space, waiting to be filled. Even when her father's clothes made their way back across the rack, what Cassie saw were the gulfs between the shirts.

The key slips easily into the old lock. After a little jiggling, the juts are so worn, the door practically opens itself. Just inside the building, Cassie flips on some of the overheads, crooked and silver, which hang like old metal ice cube trays from the ceiling.

In the chill, she slips on her blue sweatshirt. This will be a busy morning. Since there's no one else in sight, she doesn't bother with coffee. In the office, even though the delivery sheets are filled out, no one has tallied the freight, and there are no load sheets for the drivers. To save time, Cassie could add the number of bushels in her head, or jot them down on a sheet of paper standing up, but she doesn't. She sits down, finds the adding machine, and records the figures on proper tally sheets: three trucks, three drivers, and six runs, all in order. All the driver has to do is load the final number of bushels of each product, shelled clams, shucked clams, or scallops, onto the truck. Otherwise, in the rush of loading, someone will foul up the math facts he should have mastered in grade school. It's surprising how easily people lose the details, the numbers, under any kind of pressure. How come, a driver will ask, the truck is at the Clam Shack with only ten bushels? He won't know, but it's Cassie who will have to field the angry phone call and arrange for another truck.

She notes, too, the full box of old delivery sheets, not yet invoiced and in a heap. A stray elbow could knock the whole pile over, and each of those numbers is an account receivable, every bit as good as money in the bank. Biting the inside of her lip, Cassie flips her hair behind her ears, ready to work.

A pair of legs appears in front of the desk. Dodie, an older man with a full head of thick white hair who drives the Cosmo delivery truck several times a week, coughs. "We wanted an early start on the runs," he says with a rasp. "Paul's got a big date tonight." Paul, his cousin, who carries deep bags under his eyes like pouches of worry, stays a few steps behind and looks upward in mock benediction.

Cassie hands over the delivery and tally sheets and the truck keys.

"Where is everyone?" asks Paul in the mournful tone of someone who would not be surprised if told all his co-workers had passed away in the night.

Cassie shrugs. "Still sleeping."

"Nah," croaks Dodie. "Old man Cosmo, he doesn't sleep. He just keeps on ticking, like the watch."

"Where's the kid?" asks Paul.

"Needs his beauty rest," says Dodie. "Got to keep those dimples."

"David doesn't have dimples," puts in Cassie as she gets up to flick on the lights near the freezers and the loading dock.

Dodie and Paul roar with laughter and head back to the trucks.

To ignore her embarrassment, Cassie checks the schedule to find the third driver. She filled it in herself last week, but the third name is crossed off and there's no replacement. The heat in her cheeks now feels like anger. "What?" she says out loud.

David's tall frame fills in the doorway. He yawns, runs his fingers through his hair. His body gives off warmth like the heat trapped in blankets for the night, so that Cassie can't help thinking that if he'd slept in a cot in the office and just woken up, he would be just like he is now, disheveled, barely awake.

"Hello" seems too much like "Good Morning" which is too close to "How did you sleep" which feels too intimate to pass her lips, so Cassie avoids greeting him all together. "David," she reports. "We're missing a driver. Poli's crossed off the schedule."

David looks at her, surprised, and laughs out loud. Cassie narrows her eyes, suspicious of his good humor. "Do you do this to my father and uncle too?" he asks, and this is how Cassie remembers him from high school, genial and popular with the girls.

"Do what?"

"Order them around!" He throws his large, long fingers in the air and flutters them like birds.

"Of course!" she says, smiling at his beautiful hands and how they take her mind off the missing driver. She tries to remember whom he dated then, but all she can remember is that they were all tall, and one of them might have even had her own car.

"I crossed Poli off. He wanted to go to Stacy's wedding."

Stacy. Cassie has no idea who Stacy is, but apparently another Greek girl is getting married and the entire extended, enormous family will be in attendance. There would have been an engagement party, a big shower in the Hellenic community center or the church basement, an elaborate wedding with a Greek band, and then, not far off, will come the christenings.

"It's in New Hampshire. My dad and uncle are going too. At least that's the excuse they used to leave me in charge for the morning."

It isn't like old man Cosmo to go off to a wedding and leave his business untended on a busy Saturday morning. It occurs to Cassie that David is late and that he's not curious as to how she got into the building. It also occurs to Cassie that she's never been to a Greek wedding. "Is there anyone left in Ipswich who's not going to Stacy's wedding," Cassie asks, her voice sharp in the early morning, "and who knows how to drive a truck?"

"It's my fault," says David. "I'll do the runs."

She stares at David as he runs his fingers over the third delivery sheet. "What about the wedding? Aren't you going too?"

"The wedding's just a cover for me to meet all the available Greek girls in New England." He smiles and looks down.

With his head lowered over the papers, Cassie can see the photo of his grandfather behind him, the same mass of dark hair on a narrow face, the same large hands and fingers. Nicolas Cosmo was beautiful to look at.

It occurs to Cassie that if she had been Nicolas's granddaughter, she'd be standing in line to take over. But maybe not. Cosmo's daughters weren't in the business. In all the years Cassie has been working at Cosmo, she's rarely even seen them and even then, they never came inside, but stayed in their cars in the parking lot.

"Don't you want to meet all the available Greek girls?" she asks, feeling flip and hard-hearted.

David turns the delivery sheet over, but the other side is blank. Cassie makes them all one sided so there'll be no mistakes. "It's my mother who likes Greek girls. I like to make my own decisions."

Dodie's voice wheezes from beyond the doorway. "Cass! Do you need us to load up that third truck for you?" He stops when he sees David. "I guess not." As he backs up, he points his index fingers toward his cheeks and twists them in the air, a mocking grin on his face. Cassie looks down at the desk.

"I guess I'll load up the truck now and get going," says David.

Cassie glances at the small clock on the desk. You certainly should, she thinks. But he lingers and she says nothing, distracted by his good looks. David takes the sheets and leaves the office. He reappears in the doorway a few minutes later.

"Cass?" he asks her. "Would you do me a favor?"

"Sure, OK," she answers. Her heart starts to pound in anticipation.

"Could you call home and tell them I'm doing the runs so I can't make it to the wedding?"

Cassie doesn't know what wild thing she thought he would ask, but she was ready for a surprise, an opening that might allow her to bring up her plan of selling mussels to Boston maybe. She does her best to hide her disappointment. She hadn't really known him in high school. He had been two years ahead of her, a football and basketball player and always very tall. "Sure," she answers. "I can do that."

"Good," he says. "Thanks."

And he's gone. But he'll be back in three or four hours for another run. Or she'd see him tomorrow or the next day and every day for as long as she worked here because he wasn't going anywhere. He was David George Cosmo, heir to the shellfish fortune. Whereas she, Cassie, is, well, someone who's future is uncertain.

She thinks back to last semester at the community college, to Mr. Brooks and his Western Lit class, where she'd learned that she shared a name with a woman who was given the ability to see the future, along with—since it was the ancient Greeks after all—the curse that no one would believe her. She had written Mark about this because she'd written him all the time, every day sometimes, so that it got to the point that she almost forgot who she was writing to, she so looked forward to the quiet time when she could put down her thoughts for the day. Had it been that way for him too?

"It's not a curse to be able to tell it like it is, Cass," he had written back. "The world needs more of that." His reply had been comforting, had made her feel righteous even, until it had hit her that if she were really the cursed Cassandra, the curse would have to include Mark, too. He wouldn't believe her, either. This thought made her feel very alone, and it was around that time she'd started to enjoy reading the old Greeks, as Mr. Brooks put it. Each of them, left alone to battle a god or a fate over which they had no control, each waiting to make the mistake that would form, almost always ruin, the rest of their lives.

Cassie holds the phone to dial the Cosmo family to relate David's message, when she realizes that it's still before seven in the morning. The bad news about the wedding can wait until George and Eugenia have had breakfast. She turns to the safe instead, three, twenty-five, twenty-six, Greek Independence Day and the anniversary of Nicolas's death. The canvas bag is thick with money, and a quick look at all the big bills tells Cassie that either George was expecting a big haul or someone forgot to go to the bank. There must be several thousand dollars in the bag this morning and, since it's early, Cassie is considering putting it all back into the safe until the diggers show up when she hears a yell from the back.

Cassie walks toward the docks and glances at the clock over the side freezer. Andy Faragut's got several bushels, and the orange net bags lean against each other in a dangerous slope. It's too early in the tide for him to have had time to dig this many clams today.

His thin T-shirt ripples in small waves over his back, too thin for the coolers, and he's got goose bumps all over his strong, clamdigger arms. "What the hell," he says. "Let's get the show on the road."

Cassie brings out the bushel baskets, and he pours his clams in, topping off each bucket a little, as expected. It's a good haul, six and half bushels, and Cassie counts out the cash and marks the debit in her book, as well as the take. "They're yesterday's, right?" she adds as he folds the money neatly in half and puts it in the front pocket of his jeans.

He stares at her. She looks down. Of course they're yesterday's. There's too many of them, too close in time to the low tide to be today's. The shells have opened, just slightly, as if a night in a sack gave them time to relax and contemplate their new surroundings.

She shouldn't have mentioned it. She's not sure why she did.

"Who made you the FBI?" he snarls.

She looks up but he's turned away, and his shoulders are tight against his shirt. Sorry comes to her lips, but when Andy kicks an empty bucket on the way out, anger quickly washes away her contrition. It was a small mistake. Anyone else would have let it go. She needs to know. The older clams get shucked or shipped out first.

But Andy had a point. She didn't need to ask because she knew already.

By two in the afternoon, a blue sky appears, all trace of fog vanished. In this bright, dry world, Cassie takes her bike from the back of Cosmo and heads away from downtown toward Teri Pinter's house, located a few miles out in a development of similarly built new and larger homes. The air is cool but not cold, the ride runs quick and easy, and the shadows of the leaves overhead race along over the pavement like quick, small birds.

At the Pinter's, Cassie leans her bike against the deck, careful not to step on the last of the tulips, when she hears Teri and Mrs. Pinter through the screen door. Lulled by their lush and confident tones, which rise and fall, wordless, like waves, Cassie is caught listening on the porch, before she has a chance to knock.

"Cassie!" calls out Mrs. Pinter. "How long have you been here?"

"My dad said Teri called," she answers through the screen door.

"Cassie, come inside where we can hear you, dear," says Mrs. Pinter.

Cassie steps into Mrs. Pinter's neat, bright kitchen. Teri

is perched on a stool at a counter Mrs. Pinter had put in a couple of years ago so that the family could sit high up and eat their meals quickly, if they chose. Mrs. Pinter, well-dressed and crisp, coffee cup in hand, is leaning against the sink. Cassie worries that her dirty jeans and sneakers carry a vague odor of fish and, as she pushes her hair behind her ears, she sees that there's dirt under her nails.

"I just came from work," she says as an apology.

"You're still at that fish place?" asks Mrs. Pinter.

Teri smiles at Cassie. "Mom, she's probably running that fish place."

"Not exactly," says Cassie. "They brought in the grandson to do that."

"No kidding, really Cass?"

"The Cosmo family runs that business, right? An uncle and a nephew?" Mrs. Pinter starts in. "Didn't the grandson graduate a few years before you girls? Some kind of athlete?"

If Mrs. Pinter had seen his fingers work their way around the delivery sheets, she wouldn't need to ask that question. "Basketball," says Cassie. "He played basketball."

"So he just comes along and takes over?" asks Teri.

"Well, not exactly like that," Cassie answers. She perches on a rounded stool cushion, covered in a bright geometric fabric. "What are you still doing here?"

Teri looks down at her bare feet and lets out a wail. "I'm here because I should have gone to Appalachia with Donnie Stephens!"

Mrs. Pinter elaborates. "Teri's medical intern program has placements all over the country."

"It was all those stupid bluegrass records he played," continues Teri. "I just couldn't take a whole summer of those scratchy violins!"

"Teri chose to go to the Indian reservation," explains Mrs. Pinter. "And," she adds, "I believe they call them fiddles in Appalachia."

Thin and fit, wearing white shorts and a collared white shirt and holding a tennis racket, Mr. Pinter comes into the kitchen. "It's one thing to give up a research job," he says as he reaches into the closet to pull out a pair of tennis sneakers, "that pays and is close to home and to a host of medical schools to go off to gawdforsaken bits of the country to do gawdknowswhat without consulting your parents, but it's completely another to choose to work in a battle zone controlled by people with no respect for law and order." Sneakers on, he picks up his racket. "I've got to go," he says to his wife. "Bob Buckworth has a court for three o'clock." He turns to Cassie. "It's nice to see you, Cassie. You've always been reasonable. See if you can shake some sense into my daughter."

Cassie smiles, "Sure, Mr. Pinter."

"He's talking about the American Indian Movement," Mrs. Pinter explains. "It's complicated things for Teri."

"It's armed resistance," Teri says, her voice quavering. "It's not a battle zone."

"Armed resistance to what?" yells Mr. Pinter. "Doctors? A nation ruled by respect for property and not by men smoking kickapoo juice in their pipes?" He heads out the door.

"Have fun, dear," calls Mrs. Pinter to her husband. She washes out her coffee cup and puts it in the dishwasher. "The reservation cancelled the intern program."

"I can't stand him when he gets like that!" says Teri.

Cassie has always admired the Pinter kitchen. The counters are clear and the sink is always empty and clean, as if bacon or fish were never fried here. The blue and white checked floor matches the curtains over the sink, which in turn are sewn of the same material as the padded cushions.

"So, you're not going anywhere after all?" she asks Teri. As Cassie shifts on her seat, the cushion slides over the edge, but Cassie grabs the side of the counter and regains her balance. She worries what Teri thinks of David, his basketball hands and his family's business, her classes at the community college with all the kids who didn't study in high school and are back for a second or third or fourth chance. She wonders what Teri really thinks of Mark, a boyfriend just back from an unpopular war who may not be her boyfriend after all. Cassie's palms are sweaty, and she rubs them on her dirty jeans.

Teri turns to her and smiles, suddenly recovered. "Nope," she says. "I'm staying here."

Cassie remembers a project Teri did in high school, for physics class. It involved electrical wires on a board, intricately connected circuits, and various power sources. Teri had spent weeks on the wires, as usual way more time than was necessary, until the board took on an arty quality, like some type of abstract painting. Just before Teri was to present her project to the class, Bobby Paskowski rinsed a beaker he had used doing makeup work. As he turned on the faucet the water hit something unexpected in the sink and, like a tsunami, the overflow curved up and over Teri's board, soaking the circuits, turning them useless. Cassie remembers that horrified moment when no one spoke and no one dared even look at Teri. Even Mr. Webster's mouth hung open like a mackerel. "Good thing I've got a back-up in my locker," Teri finally said, to break the silence. There was an audible sigh of relief. "Really Teri?" someone had asked. "No," she'd replied. "Of course not." But she'd laughed, and she'd made it all right. Cassie is sure Mr. Webster still gave her an A.

"Can't you go back to that lab you worked at in Boston?" asks Cassie.

"They're all full for this summer. Plus, someone told the doctor I worked for last summer that I got married."

Cassie slips off her stool again. "That you got married?"

Teri laughs, and Cassie laughs too, glancing at Mrs. Pinter to include her in the fun, but Mrs. Pinter's back is turned. "Can you believe it? When I called him, he congratulated me! He seemed disappointed when I told him he was misinformed."

Cassie recalls Stu's comments about the babies on Millet Road who needed a doctor. "Maybe there's something you can do around here," she suggests. "Unless," she hesitates for fear her own glee at possibly having Teri back for the summer is interfering with her sympathies toward her friend's dilemma, "they need you in Appalachia. Or, I think they need a waitress down at the Pub. If they'd let you help out at the bar, that could be good money."

The expression on Mrs. Pinter's face would sour a lemon.

Cassie slides off her stool again. "So, what are you up to tonight?" she asks, to keep that sour lemon look off Mrs. Pinter's face. "You could come down to the Pub and talk to someone."

"Teri, under the circumstances," Mrs. Pinter says to the curtains, "it would be appropriate for you to have dinner with your great-aunt Blanche along with your father and me."

Teri puts her wrists together to imitate being handcuffed.

"That's all right." Cassie pauses, remembers Mark's face, hidden by shadows, at the Clam Shack. Teri doesn't ask about him, but Teri doesn't know he came home yesterday, since she was supposed to be gone to South Dakota. Cassie can't imagine unraveling all this in front of Mrs. Pinter. She slips off the stool once more, this time on purpose. "I got to get home and take a shower. Bye, Mrs. Pinter," she calls out, and Mrs. Pinter nods to her sink.

Cassie cruises downhill toward the main road, sees no cars, and arcs out into the street. She can tell she's tired because, as she pedals, Cassie gets that blurry feeling she gets when she hasn't had enough sleep, as if the line between her skin and the air is no longer sharp. Her movements no longer feel singular: her pumping thighs, the rubber pedals, and the whirring spokes all bleed into the space around her in a confusion of motion.

As she pulls into her own driveway and walks her bike to

the back of the house, her eyes close and she feels sleep come over her. When she opens them again, she is staring toward the train tracks, over the lot of weeds, which shift like a kaleidoscope of greens in the light breeze. Could there be little worms under the milkweed leaves, or is it too early in the season? Mark would know. She hasn't gathered them since the summer before Mark left, when the two of them had gathered worms by the dozens and made a little nursery in her kitchen, glass jars and tin foil pans filled with leaves and defecating caterpillars. She laughs to think of anything defecating in Mrs. Pinter's kitchen. Her father had just cooked around them. They were just another something on the counter, along with bills, faded newspapers, fishing line, winter gloves, and screws.

In the house, yellow afternoon light fills the kitchen, and the air is warm and close after the cool of riding her bike through the breeze. Brown bottles lie scattered on the counter and the baseball game greets her from the living room, a faint crack, quick, low voices, and the background swell of a crowd. Cassie moves toward the sounds and the darkened entranceway. As usual, her dad has the shades pulled so it's easier to see the TV, but after the glare of the outside and the kitchen, Cassie peers into the living room and can see nothing past the blur of a ball field on the screen. She looks at her father's chair, but the shaded figure in it is hunched over and leaning forward, unlike her father who likes to recline, often with his feet up. "Cassie," says her dad, "you gotta see this pitcher." Cassie looks toward the chair, but the voice is coming from the couch.

Her dad's sitting forward too, in a clean white T-shirt and baggy pants.

"Come on and watch the game, Cass," says a familiar voice from her father's chair. The tired feeling, the dark, the catch in the voice, each could have been the trigger, or maybe it was all three, but tears fill her eyes as she sits down next to her father.

"Hey, Mark," she says. She pulls the hair out her face and wipes her tears with her wrists at the same time. She is so glad to see him.

"Watch this," says her father. "Watch this guy pitch. His control is unbelievable. Mark," he barks out, "has he even come close to walking a batter yet?"

"I don't believe so," answers Mark, as if he'd sat in this same chair last Saturday afternoon and the Saturday before that, to watch the game with her father.

Maybe this is what's expected of her, that she act as if he'd never left. "What inning is it?" she asks.

"Top of the fourth," answer Mark and her dad together.

"Top of the fourth," Mark repeats.

Cassie looks at the screen. A tall, thin man lifts his right leg, knee bent and foot flexed, leans back as he brings his left arm back too, and then, in one fluid motion, the ball flies toward the plate, wriggles a bit to the right, and thump, into the catcher's mitt.

"Strike!" calls out the umpire.

The batter, it looks like Billy C., scowls and spits.

"He's mad," says Mark.

"Ah," scowls Mr. Leahy, "he's always mad about something."

Cassie laughs. "He's still mad they sent his brother to California."

"I'm still mad they sent his brother to California," snaps her father.

The pitcher—an A on his cap and Oakland written across his chest means they're playing the Athletics—grabs the ball back from the catcher and again, his right leg goes up, knee bent and foot flexed, he leans way back again as he brings his left arm back, and like water rolling over a fall, the ball flies toward the plate, inches a bit to the right; the ball curves to the outside, the batter swings, and then, smack, the ball hits the catcher's mitt.

"Strike two!" calls out the umpire.

The pitcher grabs the ball back and, as confident as if he were in his own backyard, lifts his leg up a third time, does the lean, brings the ball back, and releases it toward the plate. This time the ball buzzes straight down the middle.

"Ah! Billy just watched that go by!" calls out Mr. Leahy.

"Strike three!" yells the umpire and pumps his arm for emphasis.

The pitcher grabs the ball back and holds it a second, serene, almost smiling, a tornado of power, waiting to suck up his next victim.

"Who is this guy?" asks Cassie.

"Vida Blue," says Mark.

"Only twenty-one years old," adds his father. The same age as Mark, Cassie thinks. "They had him play a few games last year, but this year he's taken off. I've been hearing about him, but this is the first time I've seen him pitch."

"Is this the guy who carries two dimes in his back pocket?" asks Cassie. If someone asked Vida Blue why he carried those dimes, she thinks, he would most likely say he carried them for luck. She remembers Mark writing that one man in his squad carried a shark's tooth for good luck, but that Mark had carried nothing because he said that luck is a double-edged sword, and no luck went the distance. She thinks about the key in her pocket and wonders if always being reminded of what you've lost or could lose is really the flip side of a good luck charm. She wants to ask Mark what he thinks about that.

"Good," says Mark. "Yaz is up."

"He's a fish," barks Frank Leahy.

Her dad's comment shouldn't surprise Mark because her dad's always had a grudge against Yastrzemski, but Mark's enthusiasm for Yaz reveals how little he knows about this year's season.

"Mark," Cassie says, "he's been really crummy all year long. Not at all like a few years ago, or even last year."

And sure enough, Yaz swings at the first pitch, pops it up behind the plate, and the catcher snags it for the final out of the inning.

Mark gets up, beer bottle in hand. "Do you want another, Mr. Leahy?" he asks.

"Nope," waves off Frank, "but help yourself." He usually kept himself to two beers a game, sometimes less for an afternoon game.

Cassie listens as the fridge opens and the bottle top clinks onto the counter. "Do you want one, Cass?" Mark calls to her.

Cassie, surprised, turns her head around and stares at the doorway, bright with the flood of sunlight from the kitchen. Who's in her kitchen? Cassie never drank at home, rarely drank at all and, even then, only at a bar with friends. If she had more than two beers over the course of an evening, she woke up sick for the whole next day. Mark knew that. Or Mark used to know that. She wants to whisper to her father to ask him how long Mark's been here but she can't count on her father keeping his voice down when he delivers his answer.

She thinks of the pile of brown bottles on the counter. Had they been there yesterday, or had Mark drunk them all over the course of the afternoon? She watches him as he sits back down in her father's chair. Did he just teeter a bit before he let himself down? He glances at her and Cassie averts her eyes back to the TV.

It's Oakland's turn to bat, but Sonny Siebert's on the mound and he's having a good year so far. The Oakland batter, Sal Bando, is behind in the count, one and two. He fouls one into the stands to the right, another just over the Boston dug out. Mark drinks his beer from the chair and her dad's still sitting back. Siebert throws another ball, then Bando hits a weak grounder that Aparicio wings to Scott on first for the out.

"Bando can wear a pitcher down," comments Frank.

Mark, sunk in his chair, says nothing. Cassie glances over at him.

Siebert has to throw more pitches to get a batter out, but despite a base hit by Alou, the game is scoreless into the fifth.

When Blue comes back onto the screen, the three of them sit up a bit. In four pitches, he leaves Reggie snarling at the umpire. Frank Leahy is gleeful.

"Hah!" he whoops after Smith chases one over his head. "He looks like a kid chasing butterflies!"

In the seventh, when Siebert lets in a run, after an Oakland hit, a walk and a hit and run, Mark goes for another beer. This time, he doesn't offer one to anyone else one. Before Vida Blue comes back for the top of the eighth inning, Cassie gets up to survey the kitchen. There are ten empties on the counter and none left in the fridge. Her dad's been nursing the same one since the fourth, so that leaves Mark to drink the rest. Cassie comes back just as Blue strikes out Petrocelli. When did Vida Blue start carrying those dimes in his pockets, she wonders. Was it before or after he knew he could get rid of almost anyone at the plate?

When, she wonders, did Mark learn to drink ten beers and still sit straight in a chair?

In the bottom of the eighth, Kasko brings in Bolin, and the Oakland hits start to fly. Before the bleeding is stopped, the Red Sox are down by four and have yet to get past first base. Neither her dad nor Mark makes any comment during this slaughter. When they bring Blue back for the ninth, Cassie sits up, "What?" She turns to her dad.

"He can pitch the whole game, too," he answers her. "Just watch this."

Cassie leans back on the couch as Blue dispatches the

dispirited Sox batters, one-two-three. Mark has disappeared into his chair, disappeared from the room.

"That was certainly a pleasure, to watch a pitcher like that," says her father, despite the fact his beloved Red Sox, in a pennant race already, have lost the game with their top pitcher at the helm.

"Yes, sir," replies Mark. These are the first words he's spoken in innings, thinks Cassie, since she had noticed how much beer he had drunk. When her mood changed, so did his. She starts to feel guilty and then stops herself. That's ridiculous. Whatever else, he didn't come back home knowing how to read minds. He stands up. "Thank you, sir," he says to Mr. Leahy.

"You come back, we'll catch another," says Frank.

"See you, Cass," he says, and something pleading in his tone convinces her to get up and see him to the door.

His eyes, when they glance at her, are red and out of focus. "You still taking those classes this summer?" he asks her.

You're drunk, she wants to say to him but stops herself because it sounds ridiculous even to her. It's not as if she has never seen him drink too much before he left, or that she hasn't seen half of Ipswich with too much under their belts at the Pub, including Stu almost every weekend, but this is different. Drinking ten of her father's beers in a dark living room while there's a ballgame going on and she's sitting five feet away on a couch doesn't feel right.

They walk outside, and there's still a low breeze blowing the leaves overhead and the weeds in the back. The sky has turned from afternoon blue to the light blue of early evening, but Mark won't notice any of that now.

"How are you getting to your classes?" he asks her. Although his words slur a bit, he doesn't seem as tense as he had when they'd picked him up from the airport. His arms hang limp at his side, and his steps are slow.

"Same as always, the train," she answers.

"I could bring you," he says. "In my car," he adds, and this makes Cassie laugh.

"Not on your magic carpet?" she jokes.

"No," he says, serious, "I don't have one of those."

She turns to smile up at him, but he's looking down at his feet as if his sneakers are the only things that anchor him to the world and, if he took his eyes off them, he'd float away.

"Well," he says, "I promised my mom I'd come home for dinner tonight."

And this makes Cassie sad, to think of his mother, Peg, cooking dinner for her youngest son, waiting for him to come home. Would she notice a change in him? How could she not? Cassie says nothing, lets Mark amble back to his car. At the sidewalk, he stops, but instead of looking to the side for traffic, he looks up. He points his arm to the west. "The evening star," he calls out. "Cassie, can you see the evening star?" Then, still looking up, he crosses the street to his car. He sits in the front seat for what feels like a long time before he starts it up and pulls away.

Inside, she slams the kitchen door. "Dad," she calls out, but her father is already in the kitchen, clearing off the counter. "How could you let him drink so much?" She points to the paper bag of bottles in his hand. "He must have gone through almost two packs of Pabst. How long was he here?"

"Cassie, he can't have me standing over him like a mother. Besides, if he doesn't drink it here, he'll drink it somewhere else."

"You make it sound like he just came here for the beer."

"He didn't come here for the beer, Cassie."

"What did he come for then?"

He hands her the paper bag of empties. "Here, put this in the garbage on your way out. I'm in the mood for a roast beef with all the fixings from Chickie's. Why don't you get yourself a hot pastrami while you're at it?"

Cassie heads out. A screech from a wandering seagull pulls

her glance upward and the sky is backlit deep peach, and still. She looks for the evening star, but the day is still too light for her to find it. A few blocks ahead, the bright red and yellow neon sign of the sub shop flicks on, and this draws her forward like a channel marker on a dark night. She thinks of the orange sauce that goes so well with the hot pastrami, the salty taste of it and the juices that run down her wrist if she holds the bun at too much of an angle. A block or two away, a car revs up and pulls away from the curb. She turns to look, and it's Mark's car, an old green Impala, leaving a spot only twenty-five yards from her house. She stares at the receding taillights, two narrow, red eyes that turn the corner and disappear. Up in the sky, though, the peach has flipped, the way it does, all at once if you blink at the right time, to blue black, and the evening star is faintly visible a few degrees above the horizon.

## June 8, 1971

In the old brick building, the wooden floors sweat and creak in the unseasonable heat, and Cassie's forearm dews with moisture on the cheap laminate desktop. The high windows are open to the hint of an ocean breeze, a cooler wind that carries the heavy scent of creatures that thrive in dark, wet places.

Although nearly all the students wear shorts and small tops in the heat, Mr. Brooks strides in wearing what looks at first glance to be pajamas, but is really a whole suit made out of some kind of tan-and-white-striped material and his usual crisp bow tie. Cassie had Mr. Brooks last semester too, for the first half of Western Literature. School rumor has it he comes from an old, wealthy Salem family and teaches because he doesn't need the money, and because he has some kind of mental problem that makes him unsuitable for other professions.

It's clear Mr. Brooks knows a lot more than all of the ex-high school teachers who staff this community college; he often breaks off into an explanation of how the ancient Greek differs from the English translation, accompanied by five minutes of recitation in a guttural language no one's spoken for ten centuries. What is less clear is why Cassie is still studying the Greeks after one full semester, with no hope of ever leaving ancient times. Perhaps a different teacher would be onto to the next section of the textbook by now, onto something Roman or medieval, and perhaps a different teacher would wear something else beside a perfectly ironed suit to class. But a different teacher might not be able to talk about the people in the stories they read as if they were gossiping about old friends. When Hades snatches Eurydice to the underworld, and Orpheus can only retrieve her if he doesn't check back to make sure she is following him, Mr. Brooks had made them list all the reasons Orpheus would want to turn his head around. What if, in the dark, she'd tripped? What if he wants to see if she's wearing the low cut green dress that flatters her? Maybe he thinks a quick peek won't count as looking back, or maybe he's worried the ordeal has marred her looks. But then, what if Eurydice has slept with Hades and Orpheus wants to see if she looks back for her new lover? And, of course, what guarantee that Hades would keep his word?

"So many reasons to doubt!" Mr. Brooks had exclaimed. "And on what did he have to rest his faith? The love of a woman he hadn't seen in a while, the promise of a god who'd betrayed him in the first place." When the list was done, there wasn't a student left who didn't feel that Orpheus was asked to do something that was beyond his capabilities, and who didn't feel that perhaps to trust someone was a superhuman feat. After that class, Cassie had ridden home on the train feeling that the fact Orpheus couldn't help but turn his head around to check on Eurydice reflected on her, on everyone. Every important thing we are asked to do is hard for us.

And Mr. Brook's class is hard, too. Often Cassie reads the beautiful words without taking in their meaning, but with the hope that eventually this Greek world will move as easily in her head as the numbers on the accounting sheets at Cosmo.

Mr. Brooks takes out his copy of *Western Literature* and places it on his desk. "Let's talk about Odysseus as hero," he says. "You, Mr. Murphy." He points to a bearded, older kid in the front row. A lot of the students are older, or have led lives that make standard college difficult. "Be a hero for us and open some of these windows a bit more. There's a wonderful breeze outside that needs encouragement."

As the windows open wider, the breeze settles in, and the students throw out their comments.

"He was the king of Ithaca."

"He was a warrior."

"He was smart, 'the man of many wiles.'"

"He knew all the gods."

Mr. Brooks adjusts his wire rim glasses, which have slipped down his nose in the heat. "Can he be all these things and not be a hero?" he asks.

Angie, stick thin, whose jean shorts are worn and frayed at the edges, raises her hand. Cassie turns her head to watch her as she speaks. Angie, or so the story goes, went to a fancy private high school, had some trouble with heroin, and now has a small daughter. "For the first part of the book," she says, "you hear about how hard it is for Odysseus to get home. Poseidon won't let his ships cross calm waters, back in Ithaca the suitors are harassing his wife and his son. You feel sorry for the guy. And he had me convinced he had to go to Troy in the first place. They had to get Helen back because the gods messed with her head and made her run off. The Greeks had to help Menelaus get his wife back because if they don't stick together, they'll be attacked piecemeal by their enemies."

When Angie was there, she was the best in class. But she often missed weeks at a time.

"Go on, Miss Richardson."

"Well, then Odysseus starts to tell his story. He's fought nine years at Troy and then leaves to go home, right? No, he goes to Ismarus first, to visit some people friendly with the Trojans, the old enemy, and what does he do?" She opens her book and reads: "'I sacked their city, massacred their men. We took much treasure and we took their wives.' Then I begin to think . . ."

Mr. Brooks waves his loose fingers in the air, mock frightened. "That's when the trouble starts!" The class laughs. They like Mr. Brooks.

"Sure, Mr. Brooks. I begin to think, well, this man spent nine years slaughtering people, maybe he doesn't deserve to get right home. Maybe he doesn't get to come right home because he hasn't learned what he was supposed to learn."

Cassie's heart leaps to her throat like a rough lump. "What was he supposed to learn?" she asks.

"Maybe that massacring people and sacking cities is not something you should be proud of, like some kind of sport."

Craig Murphy speaks up. "Angie, that was 10,000 years ago. If men weren't good soldiers, then someone would come and sack their cities and take their wives."

"Yeah, but they sacked this other little city on the way home. Almost like an afterthought, just because they could, just because it was friendly with their big enemy, the Trojans, who they just completely wiped out. And something clicks and I say, wait a minute. Where does this end? You want to slaughter the Cicones now, and then who's next? You let these Greeks loose and there's no pulling them back. So, maybe this Odysseus, he doesn't deserve to come home."

"What's your point?" asks Craig Murphy. "It's OK that he sacked Troy because that was the enemy, but it's not OK because he sacked this other little city on the way home? Who are you to judge?"

"Angie," says Mr. Brooks, "are you making the point that warriors are responsible for their own moral conduct during a war?"

"He didn't want to go!" interrupts Cassie. "He was drafted, I mean, didn't some fancy kings come and just take Odysseus away to fight?"

"Wait," says a guy in the back, Bill, Cassie thinks his name is, but she's unsure because he is usually so quiet. She noticed him mostly because his hair is so much shorter than anyone else's. "What kind of choice do soldiers have? They're drafted and when they're sent, they have to do what they have to do."

And just like that, they've left the Greeks and gone to Vietnam. The war was always under the surface of things, waiting for a hole to thrust through. Craig is incensed. "They could go to Canada! They could refuse to pick up a gun! You can't just keep passing the buck!"

"What the hell do you know about it?" Bill stands up. "I'll tell you. You know absolutely nothing!"

Cassie looks back at Bill. The stiff way he holds his arms at his side and the way his voice is clogged back into his throat reminds her of Andy Faragut. And, she thinks, of Mark. Cassie is as sure that Bill's been to Vietnam as if he had a sticker on his forehead. Craig, however, doesn't know that some kind of line has been crossed. He's still facing forward.

"Every person's responsible for his actions," he says, matter of fact.

"War is not about sitting in some crappy classroom discussing fucking stories!" Bill has not sat down.

"Bill," says Mr. Brooks, addressing him as if he still sat quiet in the back row, "Angie says that something else is going on with Odysseus, something between the lines. Why don't you think he can get home?"

Cassie winces at his question. She can't imagine someone as angry as Bill could be interested in talking to a room full of sweaty kids and a man wearing tan and white pajamas. She waits for the outburst, but it doesn't come.

Bill slumps down and stares ahead. His voice sounds as flat and thin as hammered tin. "He's caught in some kind of nightmare and he can't wake himself up."

"What should he do?" asks Cassie in the silence that follows.

The blind lifts and lets in a light gust of air. Bill continues. "He needs something, something steady to hold onto, something that won't blow away when the winds come."

Mr. Brooks clasps his hands in front of him and looks out the window. He sighs and then begins to speak in the harsh, low tones they now recognize as ancient Greek. The sounds form a sort of rhythm, which roll over each other like waves when the rhymes appear.

The shifting sun glares through the windows, and Cassie once again has the feeling that it's not necessary for her to understand all the words as long as she holds onto the hope that some day she might.

"Jesus, Mr. Brooks. I feel like I'm at a funeral. Cut it out." This from Chris Banducci, who's in this class because the Fire Science program requires two English classes and because he wants to score high on his civil service exam next fall.

The class laughs, everyone but Bill, whose face is so set and hard that it's difficult to imagine that blood flows beneath his skin. Mr. Brooks nods at his class and then looks back out the window, quiet now, but his lips still moving, unable to stop the words from pouring out.

Outside, the hot wind shifts the leaves, the grass, and the T-shirt over Cassie's back as she strides down the steep hill, toward the main street and the train station. Cassie's taken most of the classes needed to receive her associate's degree, the highest diploma the college offers, and Mr. Brooks' classes are still the only ones that make her feel as if she's not still in high school, but rather at the beginning of understanding how little she knows.

The college is located in a small factory city that hasn't recovered from the shoe industry's exodus overseas after the last big war. Downtown is full of faded shops whose dusty window displays haven't been rotated in a decade, but empty of shoppers, and traffic is light. Cassie is not watching where she's going anyway, fixed as she is on reaching the train station benches set under full shade trees so that she can use the waiting time to read the next section of *The Odyssey*. Usually, it takes her three or four times reading through a section before she can begin to summarize what has happened with a coherence even close to what Angie seems to achieve without even trying.

A car honks once, maybe twice, before she looks to the road, to the green Chevy slowed down alongside her. Someone must be lost, she thinks at first, before she sees that it's Mark's car. What is Mark doing here, she asks herself in a panic, but collects herself and runs to the open passenger window. It is Mark's car and he is home, he is here, and she feels it inside her, how he spins her head around so that all she sees is him.

She bends down to look inside. First she sees a stranger and her mouth opens in surprise, but it is Mark, and she forces herself to smile, maybe in memory of him, but not at the cold gray face and unseeing eyes staring back at her.

She makes herself lean in the open passenger side window. He looks past her as if he knows he should look at her, but can't. "Mark?" she asks, unable to keep the question out of her voice.

"You weren't going to wait for me?"

Cassie feels dizzy. "You didn't ask me to."

"Sure, I did. You don't remember?" His fingers hold tight to the steering wheel even though the car is parked.

If this were a test, Cassie would be failing. She shakes her head back and forth.

"I told you I'd pick you up and bring you home so you don't have to take the train."

We're fighting, Cassie thinks, he's mad at me. Cassie rests her arms on the open window and bends her head forward, so that her hair flips over her face and the back of her neck welcomes the light breeze.

"You don't remember," he repeats.

He had mentioned driving her, but that was after he'd drunk

nearly a dozen beers with her father, watching the baseball game. Was she supposed to take that offer seriously?

Cassie remembers how the tiny white worms Mark plucked from her backyard weeds turned into thick green caterpillars almost overnight and how these became hot little jars of eating insects, frantic in their desire to eat, eat, always eat, so that they bit so many thin trails into the milkweed leaves that the partially eaten leaves briefly resembled green lace, until the lace was eaten away into nothing. But Cassie mostly remembers how she and Mark turned to each other, their mouths just as open and greedy, how he liked to run his hands over and through her hair.

The radio, down low, vibrates a mumble of sound in the dash. The moving leaves shuffle bits of sunlight around the hood of the car. She looks back up at him. "I remember."

He exhales, and his head falls forward. "Jesus, Cass. I guess I just freaked a bit when I thought you didn't."

She opens the door and sits on the front seat. When he makes no move to take her in his arms, she places her books on the floor of the car. In one of the many letters she wrote to him, she must have told him her summer class schedule. Maybe he's even got one of her letters in his pocket now, or maybe he memorized it.

He pulls out into the street and bottles roll and clink in the back seat. "Here you are, a college girl."

She laughs at that. The Pinters certainly wouldn't consider her a college girl. "Some college girl."

"Hey, you're almost done."

"It's only a two-year college."

"That's two years more than me."

She glances down, but the floor in front is clear of empties. "Lots of people go to four-year colleges," she says, although she knows most don't. Stu, who hadn't gone to college, has only been at White's a couple of years, and already Mr. White lets him work on the expensive foreign cars. Her senior year, the year after Mark graduated high school, Mark worked hauling lobsters. It had never occurred to him to apply to college on his own, and he had never told her he was waiting for her in order to go. They'd had plans, though, maybe they would drive across the country, maybe go to Alaska. Then, just after she graduated, he got his draft notice.

Although Mark won't look at her, he also can't keep his eyes on the road. Trees and cars catch his attention at the periphery, his head darts from side to side, and then, with a glance forward, he needs to stop, realizes too late, and slams the brakes. Cassie catches the dash palm up.

She looks at him. Sweat rolls down the side of his face, perhaps with the heat because the day is warm and, away from the water, the breeze turns stale.

Cassie does not ask him what his plans are because it is clear to her that he has none. How could he, really? He's only been home a couple of days.

The faint echoes of a song hum from the dash, and Cassie reaches forward to turn the radio up. Mark takes his hand off the steering wheel. "No, don't!" he shouts. "I don't want to hear!"

Cassie pulls her arm back into her lap. Mark never would have shouted at her like that before he went away.

The road curves along a stretch of hay fields, and the sky flattens broad on either side, like it does through the marsh. Cassie sighs into the large space and leans against the seat. She turns to Mark. "Why?"

"Why what?" he snaps.

Cassie holds her breath as if bracing for a shot. The old Mark used to have the radio on loud all the time while they drove. Outside the window, a horse barn zips by.

The road narrows and he has to slow down.

She could ask him to stop the car so she could get out. "Why don't you want to have the radio on?"

He peers at her, and this makes her nervous because he's not watching the road. "Turn it up if you want to."

She gestures forward. His head follows her moving fingers until his eyes are back on the road. "What's wrong with the radio?" she insists.

On the dashboard, the red on the odometer goes up, and the gas indicator arrow tilts below the "E." They drive by the bulb farm, almost into town. She should have him drop her off at work; it wouldn't hurt to go in a little early.

"It makes me jumpy. I don't know why." Hunched over the steering wheel, Mark looks as if everything makes him jumpy.

Cassie thinks of class, of Odysseus unable to get home, of Bill, short haired and angry and how he hissed out his words, that Odysseus was caught in a nightmare. But nightmare isn't exactly it. You can wake up from a nightmare, for one thing and for another, you have a nightmare by yourself.

"Did it make you jumpy . . . being over there?"

He shakes his head and crouches farther over the steering wheel. "It was different over there."

His head presses so far forward that it nearly touches against the glass, as if one more question would send him shooting through the window. But Cassie knows how he felt over there; he'd written her daily for over a year. "When you said that your patrol," she begins.

He turns to her, his eyes hard like glass, every muscle in his face rigid, unyielding, almost reptilian. "Don't ever-fucking-talk to me about that."

Mark swerves the car into the gas bay at the Esso and stops short. His anger pins her to her seat like manacles, but he turns off the engine and rushes out of the car. From the rearview mirror, Cassie watches him pace near the pumps, fists in pockets. The early heat fading, a raw, wet spring breeze gushes through the window and Cassie knows that when Mark returns to the driver's seat, she wants to be out of the car. She reaches for her books as Stu comes out of the garage.

He squints into the sun, runs a hand over his sweaty hair. "Hey Mark, let me get that. Hey, Cass," he adds. His head appears at her window.

Her hands shake over her books, and she keeps her head down, "Hey," she mumbles back.

Stu clanks the hose into the gas tank.

Mark stares across the street, at the shaded cemetery and the thin seventeenth-century gravestones set into the steep hill.

The pervasive scent of gas fills the car. Cassie grabs her books, gets slowly out of the car, and backs off toward the garage.

Another clank as Stu removes the hose. "The old man's a bastard with the gas," he says, "or I'd give you a tin roof."

Mark shouts, "I've been working! I've got money!"

"I didn't mean …" Stu trails off.

"Sure, you didn't." She hears the effort in Mark's voice.

Cassie and Stu watch Mark, his gaze still on the cemetery. "There they are, neat and safe, all in a row," he says.

Cassie's mother is buried in that cemetery, farther up the hill, among the newer gravestones. When she visits her grave, Cassie can see the ocean, a blue slice in the distance. At night, the view is all black.

"There's nothing neat or safe about it," she spits out.

Mark looks at her. His eyes are red rimmed as if from crying or lack of sleep. His cheekbones jut out so that she can, without much effort, imagine the skull that lies beneath his skin.

He opens his mouth; a sharp horn blasts from behind as a small blue Ford waits, impatient, behind Mark's Chevrolet for its turn at the pump.

In three quick, compact steps Mark reaches the small blue Ford parked behind, makes a grab to open the passenger door. "Come on out," he hollers.

Stu leaps over to Mark, grabs his shoulders just hard enough to throw him off balance for a second or two, and Mark takes a few steps back away from the car.

The man in the driver's seat wastes no time slipping into reverse and backing his car out of the bay. Mark chases the small blue Ford to the intersection, fists raised and bellowing, until the car turns onto the main road out of town and races out of sight.

Mark returns from the curb. Sweat rolls off his skin like water on oilcloth and soaks his shirt, even the waistband of his jeans. When he runs his palms over his head, his hair slicks down as if greased.

Cassie and Stu move toward each other. "Jesus," he says.

Mark opens his trunk, pulls out a beer, pops the top, drinks down the whole can, and reaches in for another. Halfway through the second can, he mutters curses under his breath. Despite the spring sun, goose bumps cover his arms, as if from the chill of fever. He retreats to the driver's seat with his second beer, jerks the car into reverse, and peels off.

Cassie is hit with a wave of sadness that, despite his fury, she's not in the car too. But she is also relieved.

A seagull swoops in an arc overhead, then lets out an ugly squawk.

Stu asks, "Who's the guy who turns green and big when he's mad?"

Cassie steps away from him. "Do you think you're funny?"

"The comic book man, who gets huge muscles and turns green when he gets upset?"

She is angry now.

"The Incredible Hulk. That's who," he continues. "He's a regular guy, but when something gets him really pissed he pops out of his clothes and turns into this, this monster." Stu wipes his hands on the rag that hangs from the unused belt loop. "I think he was part of some kind of science experiment gone bad."

She stares at Stu in his oversized jumpsuit. Her voice shakes. "Don't you mean Frankenstein?"

"No, Cassie. He starts out a person. Then, he'd go nuts and turn big and green, pop out of his regular clothes, go beat someone up, and then he'd go back to normal. He wasn't like Frankenstein at all."

"What happened at the end?"

"There was no end. It was a cartoon. Cartoons just keep on going."

Another horn blast calls Stu back to the pumps to fill up a station wagon. Cassie leaves while his back is turned; she doesn't know what to say.

She remembers a late night at the beach, just before Mark had to leave. Even though the sand held in the heat of the day, the slightest breeze raised the bumps on their skin. Not a light, not a shout, not an airplane overhead, just the lap of the waves on the wet shore and the blue dunes under the moon. But she didn't feel alone with Mark. She felt tiny, hidden for the moment by the last free, empty place, hidden by the sand and the waves, with the rest of the world hovering over them in the night, waiting for them. "I'm not going," he said to her. "I just won't go." "Shh, shh," she said, but not out of comfort. She meant, shh, don't say it out loud, they're listening.

## June 10, 1971

Cassie pedals toward Cosmo. The quiet street, the spring bright sun, the day carries a stillness so that she feels as if she were bicycling in place while the world rolls slowly by on a screen.

A police car parks at a slant across Cosmo's front gravel lot. The front door, wide open, blasts air-conditioned air into the sultry noon. Cassie leaves her bike, enters the building, and closes the door behind her. Inside, all of the overhead bulbs are on; the narrow beams of illumination strung between metal crosshatches from the ceiling cut into the usual gloom. In the excessive light, the corrugated metal walls bend into shadows and the interior takes on an odd, wavy atmosphere, at once dizzying and unnerving.

Doors left open, lights all on, Cassie hurries toward the office. The last crisis at Cosmo was four years ago, when George jammed his fingers in the forklift while disentangling a reluctant box. Cassie, just hired as a clam shucker, stood on the wet floor and turned her head with the others toward the harrowing scream. Unlike the others, she ran toward the emergency and, with a memory of a pen-and-ink sketch of a Girl Scout in glasses wrapping a long strip of gauze around a boy's elbow, she tore the end of George's sleeve away from his bloody and gashed hand, wrapped the wounds up in towels scavenged from the bathroom, and held the bandages tight until Dodie arrived to take him to the hospital. After that day, Cosmo plucked Cassie from the shucker's station, increased her responsibilities, and raised her wages.

Although Cassie worries first about the old man, it's in David, his hands cupped over his elbows, his height sending shadows fifteen feet behind, that the trouble rests. David sees her first and his eyes, brown and warm and beautiful, stand out in his nervous face for an instant before he speaks. "Cassie's here."

Cosmo looks up at her, his round face a moon of calm. George turns in her direction. Something hard in his face makes Cassie uneasy. She wonders, not for the first time, why the old man is the most grateful to her when it was George's fingers that she saved.

"Finally," says Cosmo. "She can tell you what happened." George offers no greeting, perhaps because he has to step aside to make room for the cop and his wide gun belt to push out the narrow doorway of the office.

"Cassandra Leahy?" the cop asks her, his voice large. His precise moustache is gray, while the hair on his head is a dapper kind of black. "A sum of money was taken from the safe in the office of Cosmo Shellfish. According to the owners, you were the last person to have access to the safe."

The old man waves his hand at the cop, as if he were pushing away the smell of burnt toast. "Cassie," he says, "we just need to know how much was left on Saturday."

They're asking her to tell them how much was taken. A flare of annoyance shoots through her; how many times had she warned George that his preference for cash payments to the clammers would bring trouble? "I can tell you what I paid out on Saturday."

"That's in the books," says David.

George says something in Greek.

Was it something not meant for the cop or something not meant for her to hear? She turns to the old man. "I didn't count what was there."

She remembers the pile of money, how it swelled the canvas bag, so much of it that someone must have missed a bank run. Although George used to go to the bank, maybe it's David's job now, because George would never miss a bank deposit.

"It must have been at least five hundred," Cassie says finally.

"How do you know this?" The cop's eyes, hard and glittering over his fancy moustache, make her careful with her words. Does he think she took the money?

"From handling the cash. You get a sense."

"According to David Cosmo, the doors were locked when he arrived, and he locked them when he left, at approximately three-thirty Saturday afternoon."

Cassie opens her mouth to say, wait, I was in here first on Saturday morning, the lock was weak and I used my house key to get in. She glances at David, who looks at his shoes, large sneakers with bright red stripes, as his lie is recounted. But, under the unnaturally bright overheads, the absurdity of breaking into her own workplace hits her and she can't find the words to explain herself. What had been her hurry?

The cop doesn't wait for an answer. "I need a list of everyone who came in the building between Friday and Saturday afternoon, any names of troublemakers or suspects. With no sign of forced entry, it could have been an inside job." He turns to retrieve his hat off the desk.

After the cop heads for the door, George sighs and runs his palms through his thick, white hair. He faces Cassie, accusatory. "Where were you? We tried to call you all morning."

Does George think she took the money? "I was at school."

George snaps, "Aren't you done yet?"

She does not want to explain to George, with David and Cosmo listening, why she's into her third year of a two-year program. "Summer classes," she mumbles.

"You don't need any of it now," comments the old man.

Cassie starts to ask him what he means by that but George

interrupts.

"Where's the goddamn coffee?" George retreats to the back. Lights snap off overhead as he restores the hut to its usual shade. "Hah!" his voice sounds like a foghorn in the dark. "I want a five hundred dollar cup of coffee!"

David turns, heads toward the back after his father.

Cosmo nods to her. "It's a lot of money," says Cassie.

"Five hundred dollars is five hundred dollars," answers Cosmo. He speaks in Greek, then in English; "They give it to you, they take it from you." He heads toward the shucker stations but turns back. "Cassie," he says, "you know any crazy people?"

She thinks of Mark, hands in the air, running toward the scared man in the blue Ford. In that state Mark could have done anything, maybe even broken into Cosmo and stolen money. "I don't think so," she answers.

"A crazy person came in here and took the money." He looks at her, as if considering something, and then follows his nephew.

Water swooshes over the bays, and Cassie looks into the office. The safe door is wide open and the floor strewn with papers. Cassie retrieves the mugs. First she'll make coffee.

In the side room that serves as a kitchen, Cassie rinses out the mugs, letting the warm water burn her chilly fingertips. Someone touches her shoulder, runs his hand up and down her arm. She closes her eyes, Mark, but it's been a long time since Mark has touched her.

David bends down, his lips near her ear. "Thanks for covering for me."

She steps away and shakes her head no, I didn't cover for you.

"I just didn't want to hear another lecture from my father about my work ethic." David speaks these last two words in a singsong. He steps away from her. With a jab of insight, Cassie realizes that she is trapped because using her house key to get into work cannot be seen in an innocent light. Since she hadn't told the cop or Cosmo or George that she was the first to be at work on Saturday when she was asked, her one chance to tell the truth has come and gone.

The water runs in the sink behind her. She should go right now, before any more time passes, and tell Cosmo that she let herself into the hut with her own house key, that she was too embarrassed to confess this in front of the cop.

David slips from the room.

Why hadn't she trusted Cosmo, of all people, with her little story about the key? With a ping of embarrassment, Cassie knows that somewhere in the Cosmo family discussion, they must have considered that she could have taken the money; even if they immediately dismissed it, it must have been brought up.

In the office, uneasy, Cassie sets up the coffee and gathers the scattered paperwork. The mess isn't as bad as it looked at first, probably because anyone would know that whatever was of value would be in the safe. She hesitates before she shuts the safe door, why would Cosmo ask her if she knew any crazy people? Would he consider Mark a crazy person? The door shuts with a click; the safe will need new numbers.

George returns to the office and briefly, Cassie wants to tell him the truth. "George."

"You're right," he snaps. "I'm going today to order the checks."

"I wasn't going to say, I told you so."

"No more cash, no more talk about it." George kneels down by the safe to set a new combination.

She spots David moving in the gloom beyond the office door. What if he comes clean about coming to work late on Saturday? Where would that leave her? She has no recourse. She is just going to have to trust that he doesn't. Cassie feels sneaky though, and being dependent on his goodwill feels as safe as a dry sand bar in a rising tide.

Later that afternoon, Cassie throws up into the gravel. At the edge of the parking lot nearer the street rests a large maple, and Cassie plunks down on the small patch of grassy weeds under its generous shade and closes her eyes. She shouldn't have skipped lunch and then drunk so much coffee.

Teri had asked if she'd waited for Mark to come home. Of course she had. With their letters trading back and forth for two years, she'd told him more than she would have if he'd been here, more than she would have even told herself. Now, the letters had stopped coming, and Mark is back. But where was the person who'd written the letters? The person she'd fallen in love with all over again? Maybe he doesn't exist.

She bends her head over to gag. A distant wail signals the approaching train. In a few moments, a stream of commuters will pass on the sidewalk a few feet away. Cassie leans against the trunk, places her palms on the weeds, and pushes herself up.

**June 12, 1971**

Sometimes the stories float inside her.

As Narcissus smoothes the silver surface of the moonlit pond, searching for his face, his fingers scramble his image into a thousand pieces, like a broken windshield. With Leda, it is always noon and very hot, and the reeds whisper around her. Perhaps the girl had given the swan a look with her mouth half open, or passed her hands over her breasts, thinking she was alone with the birds before one pressed her down onto the porous damp earth, thick with the roots of plants, and then glided back off onto the water. Now, one black-hulled ship heads home after ten years of war, smothered in fog, the waves slapping against the bow in the dead silence.

But this ship has a bell, an insistent clanging from far away as Frank Leahy drops the heavy frying pan into the sink. The smell of cooked eggs mingles with a bedroom already hot in the early summer sun. Cassie rolls over onto her warm pillow, pushes her damp hair back from her forehead, and glances at the clock, not even six thirty.

She wonders if she caught Mark at the beginning of his day, whether he would be easier to talk to. Cassie dresses and heads for the kitchen.

"Hello, early bird," says her father. "There's no morning tide."

"I know," she answers and leaves it at that. Two people can't live in the same house for too long if they don't keep things from each other.

Her father piles four bacon slices on buttered toast, slips a fried egg on top, and lifts the pyramid to his mouth, like a slice of pizza.

Dressed for work in a heavy blue work shirt and heavy blue pants, he won't walk out of the backless house slippers until his feet are out the door. Frank goes through a pair a year, and each Christmas brings a replacement from Cassie. As Frank bends over his breakfast, the morning sun shines behind him, and Cassie notices that the black hair on top of her father's head is thinning away from the edges. To Cassie, her father has always been the same age, but then she's seen him every day of her life. It follows that, if she went away and came back, he would be older.

"You want coffee?" he asks. She shakes her head. Just the thought of the hot liquid on this hot morning makes her stomach queasy, and she puts down her toast. Frank takes the pot off the stove and pours himself a cup. "I talked to a couple of my buddies about that break-in," he says as he passes her a full plate.

Frank has contacts in the police, the fire station, the department of public works. He could have gotten information while at Marty's getting doughnuts, or at the boatyard, or at the VFW bar.

Cassie slides a slice of bacon through the broken yoke. She wants to know if anyone thinks she took the money. "The old man thinks a crazy person broke in and took it." She pictures Mark running after the blue Ford. "You know, like a druggie or something."

Franks sits back down. "Yeah, well, the cops think it's an inside job, no sign of forced entry, the mess in the office not really a search, just made to look like one."

"That front door basically has no lock on it. And George keeps all this cash around."

"Do many people know that?"

Cassie lifts her eyes from her plate to glance at the kitchen around her. Newspapers and fishing gear litter the counter, dishes sit in the sink. The yellow walls are bright with the eastern sun and so are the yellow curtains over the window. "What do you mean?"

"Well," he adds as he layers another slice of toast and lifts it to his mouth, "you're working in a family business. You're the only one in that joint who's not family."

"I've got a Greek name."

"Jesus, Cassie."

"You know what it meant to the Greeks, where it comes from?"

He chews the last of his breakfast, drinks down his coffee. "It comes from your mother. She liked the way it sounded." He gets up from the table to put his dishes in the sink. "I don't know anything about the Greeks."

"Dad, I mean the ancient Greeks, not the Cosmo family!"

He runs water over the dishes. "I don't give a shit about the ancient Greeks, but I do know that no one's looking out for you over there."

"The old man is."

"The old man is getting on."

The clock on the stove reads four after seven. Cassie pushes her father away from the sink. "Go away, I'll do these."

"I don't want any steel wool . . ."

"On the frying pan. I know." She runs the water until his car pulls out of the driveway and then leaves the dishes in the sink to soak.


Ed and Peg Harris have lived forever at the east end of town, out with the summer cottages. The road out is empty of houses, of trees, even of bushes, just a thin line of pavement through three miles of marsh. During big storms and extra-high tides, the ocean seeps in from both sides and leaves the road impassable for hours at a stretch. In the winter, when the marshes are dead and flat and coarse, the sky is gray, and the wind whips in with no barrier off the sea, it feels like pure desolation.

Today, however, the ocean is merely two tiny blue strips on either side of the road, beyond the grasses, in the distance. Great puffs of white clouds circle Cassie's head, and from below rises the easy scent of salt and hay and early summer morning, sharp but not overbright. Too early for insects, the wind whooshes in an undertone, flattening the tips of the sea of bright green marsh grass in rolling waves. In the quiet, Cassie hears the bike tires turn against the macadam, the marsh heron flap the air into flight, and her heartbeat.

Just before the flats rise into the slightly wooded island, the ocean curves into the side of the road, and the high tide laps at the rocky beach. Cassie rides up the road around to where the Harris's house clings to the side of a hill that slopes down into the water. The house looks west over the tidal river that threads its way north through the grasses into the ocean bay, and east to the road.

A tan sedan sits in the driveway, next to Mark's green Chevy, but the front door to the house is closed. "Hello," Cassie calls. "It's me, Cassie!" The ocean sucks up sound, and the wind carries it, but Cassie hears a faint reply that she follows around the house to the backyard, which, since it looks out on the water, feels more like the front.

A heavy green hose lies loosely coiled under the spigot. Flower beds by the back door look freshly turned, and bags of cow manure rest in the tall weeds just beyond the edge of the lawn. A ten-by-three-foot strip of dirt holds tiny plants, the vegetables. The lawn is not the perfect lawn you see on bags of grass seed, but the yard has a hum of busyness and production. Despite the hardness of the last year, a brisk sanity rules.

Peg Harris comes from around the stairs carrying a flat of pink impatiens. The light breeze floats wisps of her gray hair, like spider webs around her face. She smiles when she sees Cassie, but Cassie has to force herself to smile back, she's so taken by the deep lavender circles under Peg's eyes. She hadn't noticed them the last time she'd seen Peg, when they'd gone to pick up Mark at the airport.

"I'm behind with my planting," she says. "These poor things have been ready to go for weeks. Just look at them, they're growing out of their pots." She turns the flat upside down and the plants fall out in tight balls, all the stray soil bound by roots. Peg has grown her own seedlings for as long as Cassie has known her, in orderly rows under bright lights in the basement.

"Do you need any help?" Cassie asks.

"Oh, no," Peg replies as she kneels by the bed. "I turned this over a few days ago. All I have to do is pop them in."

Cassie sits on the back steps, which lead up to the kitchen.

"How's your dad?" asks Peg.

"He's fine, thanks," answers Cassie.

"I always wonder he didn't find someone." This is one of Peg's favorite topics. "He was always so handsome and a steady earner too."

"He still could," says Cassie, but she doesn't mean it. Where would he find her? At the K Club? Fishing in the bay? At the A&P? Well, maybe there, searching for soft spots on the green peppers.

Peg laughs. "He's just waiting for you to get out from under his feet."

Cassie looks toward the bottom of the hill, over the brush that divides the yard from the water. Little ripples on a flat surface signal currents in the changing tide, and a lone seagull circles above. Although she and Peg have never had a heart-to-heart, there was never a reason to before. Cassie guesses that she thought, when Peg Harris saw her come in the door, that Peg would sit her down and they could talk about all the ways Mark has changed and what they could do to bring him back. She was his mother, after all. How could she not notice and worry?

The kitchen door opens and Ed Harris slams a cardboard box full of bottles onto the back landing. Cassie turns to look, but Peg continues to dig small, even rows of holes into the dirt with her spade. Ed's face, tight with concentration, breaks into puzzlement and then a smile at Cassie. "Early morning cleaning," he says.

Cassie knows the box is full of beer bottles, and she knows who drank them. She returns the smile. "Hi, Mr. Harris."

"Well, I'll be off," he says. "Peg must have told you that Mark's not up yet." Ed Harris tightens the knot of his thin black tie. He's sold large appliances at Sears for almost thirty years. "He sleeps late now."

"Sure, Mr. Harris," says Cassie.

Ed Harris starts down the stairs, and Cassie scoots over to the side of the lowest step to let him pass. Near the bottom, he trips. Although heavyset, Ed Harris is agile, and he manages to flail his arms and kick his legs so that he lands almost on his knees in the grass, before turning over quickly onto his back, where he rests, breathing short, shallow gasps.

Peg stands over him, still in her gardening gloves. "It'll be fall before I get my flowers in!" She reaches down and pulls at her husband's uninjured hand. "Let's go, before you're late for work as well."

He groans, pulls himself up, and spends a moment bent over, collecting himself. When he faces them, Cassie says, "Mr. Harris, your hand's bleeding."

He waves off Cassie's ministrations. "Peg," he says, maybe in order to lighten the mood, "Peg, you gotta stop putting those banana peels on the steps!"

In a flash of irritation, she knows that these people will be no use to her. She doubts if they have even spoken to each other about the changes in their son, so accustomed they are to good cheer and happy faces.

She sighs and follows them up the stairs. Their kitchen is not yellow; rather it was built with what was at hand. The walls are blue, but the floor is white, and the curtains green. The counters are clear and clean, so that Cassie isn't sure whether breakfast is long over or hasn't yet been made. Facing west as it does, the morning light is low and cool, but Cassie remembers brilliant orange sunsets over the water beyond the windows over the sink and beyond the window on the floor below, where Mark must lie, still sleeping in the walk-out basement built into the hill.

Peg runs her husband's hand under the faucet and asks Cassie for a band-aid, which she retrieves from the medicine cabinet in the bathroom.

What she really wants to do now is to sneak down the stairs, crawl into Mark's narrow bed, and pull herself up against his back so that the when he wakes, all he would have to do is turn around to take her in his arms.

She heads outside. Two or three leftover impatiens lie on their side by the dug holes. Peg will be sure to plant them before the morning is over. Then she'll most likely water them every day, on schedule, so that they grow big and strapping.

Ed and Peg clump down the stairs. "Don't be a stranger, Cassie," Ed calls to her as he rounds the yard to his car, while Peg bends back to her flowers.

Cassie hesitates at the bottom step, but when she follows Ed Harris around the corner, Peg's smile betrays relief at finally having some time to plant her neglected flowers and no one to interrupt her or ask her any questions.

When Ed Harris's car is out of sight, Cassie returns into the house by way of the front door, rarely used but never locked. She sneaks like a thief down the steps to the basement where Mark sleeps, closing each door behind her with quiet clicks. A slight air of mildew greets her as she descends the steps. Little light reaches the dark paneled hall and Cassie keeps to the side until she reaches Mark's room. At his door, she hesitates. In the old days, she would have surprised him out of sleep. In the old days, however, she wouldn't have snuck into his house.

She knocks lightly. The hollow door, not shut tight, shifts in the jam. Cassie pushes it open.

Dank, stale beer and sweat foul the air, the light filtered blue through the heavy curtains. "Mark!" she whispers. In the half-light, mounds of what might be dirty clothes or towels litter the floor. "Mark?"

"Over here." He is sitting on the floor, in the corner, half shielded by a dresser.

"I thought you were sleeping."

"I don't sleep."

Outside, Peg Harris's garden trowel hits a rock with a clank.

"What are you doing?"

He shrugs and sighs.

"Meditating?" she jokes.

"You don't know. They take that shit really seriously over there. Altars and food and shit."

Cassie moves toward him, trips over something on the floor. She reaches to the window just to the left of where he sits. "How about a little ..."

"No!" His hand reaches out and grabs her ankle, tight and unforgiving.

"Ow!" She starts to shake him free and he lets go.

"Oh God, I'm sorry," he rasps, his shoulders shaking lightly up and down, his breath coming in hoarse crescendos.

"Mark ..."

"Go away!" he whispers.

"But ..."

"Go away!" he shouts. "Go away! Go away! Go away!"

Gardening just a few feet away, Peg must hear the outburst.

Shame seeps rapidly into Cassie, and she turns to race back

up and out of the house.

Peg Harris greets her at the top of the stairs. For a split second her look is hard, almost triumphant, as if to say, hah, you can't get through to him either, but then, in a blink, she smiles at Cassie. "Mark's up! Wonderful, now I can fix some breakfast." She turns quickly back to the kitchen.

Cassie leaves the way she came, out the front door and into the bright blue morning.

## June 15, 1971

Cassie pedals down High Street, a wide drive lined with houses built centuries before. Just as she nudges her handlebars toward the street that brings her home, a truck approaches in the oncoming lane, cutting off her turn. On a whim, rather than swing back she heads on. When she reaches the high school, she turns in the drive and rides over the grass to the field and leaves her bike on its side.

The field is empty, as is the parking lot. As she walks onto the track, her footsteps on the gravel echo between the bare bleachers that circle the track like a skeleton.

She does a few preliminary stretches, and then she runs. Exhilaration fills her for the first quarter turn and what's left of the cool morning air braces her skin. Too quickly, her sneakers seem to gain weight as her muscles rebel against the unnatural exercise. Into the second turn, her lungs come up short and with that, exhaustion seeps into her legs and arms. But into the third, a rhythm, born of steadiness and habit, guides her. Ragged though it is, she forces a mile and a half. She manages a little over two miles before her stomach roils, and she collapses onto the grass, her mouth watery. Her body's spent, but the few moments she spends on her back in the grass, arm slung over her forehead, are full of relief.

I can do this every day, she tells herself. I'll need new sneakers, though, something lighter, with the sole still padded and fresh.

Back on her bike, she stands as she crosses the grass, calves strong enough but thighs weak, wind off, with some dizziness. Her tires flatten a little as they roll back over the curb. She should stop by the Esso and get some air.

By the air pump at the gas station, she kneels to unscrew the metal cap. Her fingers shake a bit, but Cassie fits the hissing hose on the opening without looking around for Stu. He appears, though, like a sentry.

"What's with you?" he asks. "You're all red."

She moves to the next tire. "I was running up the track."

"Way to go Cass," he says.

She looks up at him. "You think so?"

He nods, arms crossed. "I do."

She screws the cap back onto the second tire, smiling at her shaky fingers. If she were serious, she would need to work with weights again. "Thanks, Stu."

He rubs his fingers over the rag that hangs from his unused belt loops. "Air is free."

## June 17, 1971

Cassie finds Teri at one of the small tables that ring the bar at the Pub, seated with a stranger. The stranger, a beautiful girl with a forbidding face, has the long, loose hair that's in fashion, but with none of the sloppiness that comes with a hippy lifestyle. Hers falls neatly away from her blue eyes and curves down her back in a precise half circle. Earrings heavy in turquoise and silver hover over bare shoulders, and her boots have tiny stitched star patterns worked into the leather. Cassie pulls her own unkempt hair back behind her ears and wishes she'd worn anything but her too-comfortable faded red shirt. Teri, with her sensible short, frequently trimmed hair, waves and moves her chair so Cassie can join them at the small table.

"Cassie, this is Nina Cassidy, from school. She's visiting for a few days before she heads to Italy."

Nina glances at Cassie and nods slightly. She has none of the typical girls' eagerness to please about her.

For Teri's sake, Cassie remains polite. "Are you part of the intern program too?"

"Of course not!" interjects Teri. "She's going to Italy, with her uncle, for the summer."

"Of course," Cassie says. The only people she knows who have ever been to Europe are some of her father's friends, sent there in World War II, but they don't talk much about it. She slips back off the bar seat. "I'm going to get a beer."

A cloudy mirror streaked with thin gold lines reflects the

boisterous crowd. The older men in white T-shirts who come for dinner are gone, and those remaining are young and ill dressed. The sweet smell of marijuana snakes its way through the cigarette smoke. Cassie turns toward the scent, and looks over the half wall to the pool table. She catches a glimpse of Stu, and then, looking thin in new jeans and a baggy olive green shirt, she spots Mark, leaning over the green felt, cue in hand. All right then, she says to herself, he made it out of the basement with no help from me.

She hesitates at the bar. If he really wanted to avoid her, he should have gone somewhere else. Maybe Stu even told him that she'd be here.

But, so far, Mark's stranded her at the Esso and thrown her out of his room. Cassie isn't used to being on the seeking side of a relationship, and the uncertainty of it saps her confidence and her pleasure.

Cassie glances back at Teri and Miss Italy, a half wall and twenty feet away, and fights the inclination to leave the Pub, to go out into the dusk and home again, where maybe her father is home watching the same ball game that's playing on the TV over the bar.

She decides to wait. Mark can't leave the Pub without walking out the poolroom door. When Cassie returns to Teri and her friend, she sits so that she is mostly turned to the crowd around the pool table and the bar behind. She takes a quick sip. The beer is bitter but cold, so drinkable.

"So, this is your haunt," remarks Nina. Her tone, bored yet commanding, makes Cassie sit up straighter in her chair.

Teri laughs. "Yes. Cassie's dating the bartender."

Nina looks curiously over toward the bar.

"I'm joking," says Teri.

Nina shrugs, twists one of ten silver bracelets on her arm.

Her arms look unused, with no visible muscle beneath her smooth tan skin. Teri and I were the only girls in chemistry class, Cassie thinks; we were the only girls in physics, too.

"Are you going to be a doctor too?" she asks Nina.

Nina laughs. "Oh no. I just took anatomy for a Michelan-gelo, da Vinci kind of reason. You know. The cadavers and all. I'm into cadavers." She lifts up her arms and turns her hands back and forth. The bracelets clink. "Dead bodies! From the inside out!" Her blue eyes rest briefly on Cassie before they turn toward a burst of shouting that comes from beyond the half wall, near the pool table.

"Ooh!" Nina gushes and slides off her stool. "There's a pool table! I haven't played since school got out." As she heads for the smoke of the back room, her long skirt sways just slightly over her styled boots, and her hair falls prettily down her back. The crowd parts in front of her. No one else looks like her here, so polished, so sure of herself.

"Isn't she fun?" asks Teri. "She'll do anything."

Fun isn't the first word that comes to Cassie, but she smiles anyway as she watches Nina enter the poolroom and stand for a few minutes by the game in progress. Before long, a tall, bearded man gives her a beer, and she's holding a cue. When she bends to hit the ball, every man in the room, Stu and Mark included, stares at her long, mostly bare back. They all look away as she steps back from the table, everyone but Stu. By the way Nina flips her sleek blonde hair over her shoulder and takes her beer back, Cassie knows that Nina understands she's the center of attention. What must it be like, Cassie wonders, to have people notice you whenever you walk into a room?

"Has she been your friend a long time?" Cassie asks.

"I just met her this semester, in Anatomy. She's really an art major and took the class for drawing, like she said, so she's different than most of the people in my premed classes. Yesterday she called and invited herself down. The funny thing is, my parents already love her. Everywhere she goes, she knows just what to do. I mean, I didn't even know she played pool."

When Nina drifts over to Mark, jealousy stabs Cassie. Mark looks down at his shoes, or maybe at Nina's boots. He looks harder to Cassie, less fleshy than the men around him, and someone who didn't know better could mistake this for handsome. Cassie wants to race to the poolroom to put herself between them, but the perfection of Nina's hair in a precise oval across her naked back stops her. After what seems to Cassie like a very long time but is probably only a few minutes, Nina flips her hair and walks away from him. Eyes still down, Mark reaches for a beer, but before he moves away from her, he turns back, head up, and watches her retreat.

"What are you party poops still doing here?" Nina sits down and adjusts her halter top, which has slid to the side, leaving one breast almost bare and the other smothered. "What a crew in there. They tried to tell me that one guy just got back from Vietnam, can you imagine? As if anyone's still going."

"They're still drafting people," says Cassie.

"So I went over to check him out and you know what?" She leans her head toward the table and lowers her voice. "He lost his thing over there and so now he can't have a girlfriend."

Cassie wants to push Nina off the stool.

Before she has a chance to, a shout rises above the din of the bar, followed by angry cries, cracking, and smashing glass. Conversation stops, and in the lull the jukebox sings "American Pie," the part where the beat speeds up and Don McLean asks who wrote the book of love and do we have faith in God above, as shouts and grunts and more crashing come from the poolroom. The bartender, a burly man, comes out from behind the bar holding a bat. He shouts, "Outside boys! Take this one outside!" Cassie wonders if he's heard this in a movie, or whether some people are born able to take charge. A momentum of tussling bodies works its way past the bar as people scurry out of its path. Mark is shoved from behind, his arms punching wildly, and Stu has someone else by the arm. Cassie, Teri, and Nina all stand tight against the wall, but by the time the mob reaches their table, the men are running for the door.

"Primal," says Nina. "I like it."

"Wasn't that Mark?" Teri asks Cassie. "And that other guy?"

"No, I'm sure it wasn't," answers Cassie.

Teri, head tilted and eyes narrowed, stares at her. She feels like something under a microscope. "I have to use the bathroom," Cassie says and excuses herself from the table.

Just beyond the bathroom swirls a burst of fresh air from the open front door, and beyond that a soft breeze plays with the leaves of the young trees planted on the sidewalk out front.

Outside, the fighters have scattered, probably in worry that the police would show. Maybe Mark hasn't gone that far.

Cassie walks along the edge of the building, down the block, toward the first of a series of alleys that lead toward the back lots that border the river. Outside the bar, the block is quiet, made up mostly of the newspaper store, some small shops, and a bank, all long closed for the day. She walks to the edge of the alley and peers down what part is illuminated by the streetlights.

"Mark!" she half whispers. The alley smells dank, like the river and the sea that mixes with it a quarter of a mile downstream.

"Cassie!" She can make out some movement in the shadows, Stu. "Who's the blonde with the boots?"

"What?"

"Come on, you know, the cute one playing pool with us."

"Forget it, she's going to Italy with her uncle."

"Damn. Why don't any of your friends stay in one place?" He steps into the half-light thrown by the streetlamp. His left eye is swollen shut, and a trickle of blood is dried on his cheek.

"What happened to you?"

He smiles and winces. "Ran into a fistful of fingers."

"You should clean that up."

"We're waiting for the cops to clear first."

"Is Mark back there?"

"He was a minute ago."

Cassie holds one palm against the brick wall to guide her. As she moves down the alley, the shallow river gargles the loose stones of the bed as it moves toward the sea, drowning out the sounds from the street behind, and the dank, muddy smell of the riverbank chills the air. Now so dark she can't see her own feet, Cassie stops when the pavement ends, where the ground is soft and moist.

"Boo!"

As if a fist locked around her throat, Cassie cannot even scream when someone steps out, grabs her about the shoulders, spins her back, and pushes her roughly against the wall. He smells like beer, and maybe it takes all day for him to drink enough to be able to hold her, but Cassie puts up no resistance. His familiar hands and arms pull her in like taking her home. She's been waiting a long time.

Afterward, he leans against her, the river gurgling suddenly again in the background. The bricks she leans against are cold, and she shivers. She pulls him back against her hips. "Did you tell Nina you lost your equipment?"

He laughs into her hair. "Stu made that up because he wanted to get into the blonde's pants." Cassie remembers Stu, wonders briefly where he is.

"Don't be mean," she teases.

"What?" Mark continues. His tone is mocking. "Did you worry?" His lips crawl, wet and needy along her neck, toward her ear. He presses her against the brick wall, urgent. "Cass," he whispers, "what are you afraid of?"

He is rougher than she remembers.

"Are you afraid of me?"

She can barely shake her head, no.

"Boo!" he says, not loudly, but an electric jolt of fear runs through her. She turns her head away, but he cups it gently in his hands.

"I'm serious, Cass."

"I don't know," she whispers, but he's right; fear crawls in the dark behind Mark and arches her nostrils in the dank of the unfamiliar, muddy fresh water. It rubs the inside of her belly like a moving snake, in serpentine waves of tightness.

Her lips are so close to his and she kisses them, then his nose, his cheek, his eyebrows. She has missed him so much.

"What are you afraid of?" she asks into the side of his neck, which smells of sweat and beer and smoke.

He shivers and tenses, tries to move away, but she holds onto him. "It's your turn," she whispers.

He buries his head into her neck. "I can't stop what's running in my head, like the same movie over and over." She can barely hear him. "Please." He lifts his face and presses against her hair. "Please don't leave me alone."

She wraps her arms around his back. "Why would I ever want to do that?"

Stu reappears. "Sorry, but the cops are driving down the street real slow, and I had to duck back here." He leans against the wall next to them.

"Hey, Cass, did that blonde say anything about me?"

Mark laughs. She feels it heave out of his chest. Cassie thinks this may be the first time she's heard him laugh since he's come home. "Jesus, Stu."

"Nina said you were primal," Cassie tells Stu.

"What the hell does that mean?"

Mark snorts. "She wants primal? I'll show her primal." His words are like metal teeth. Cassie considers that it's not Nina's fault she has an uncle who takes her to Italy, just like she can't help her smooth yellow hair or nice boots. "Shit," he relents, "listen to me."

"Nina meant it like she likes it," says Cassie to Stu. "Maybe you should go back in there with your cut eye and growl at her."

"Nah, Harry's not going to let us back in until he cools down, might take a week or so. But Cass," he turns to her, "maybe you could invite them down to our alley, we could throw a little party here."

Cassie thinks of Teri. Although Nina might like this little dark corner, Teri wouldn't. Teri doesn't need dark corners for excitement, or exploration.

A siren goes off briefly. Cassie feels Mark turn to stone in her arms. He turns from her and peers around the corner, into the dark.

Cassie looks toward the river, where small reflections of light bounce on the water in the running tide.

"It's only the cops," says Stu.

Mark lets his hand fall and something metal clinks against the brick.

"What's that?" Cassie asks.

He lifts his right arm up and points ahead. "Pow!"

Cassie's mouth parches. Where had he been hiding a gun? In the pocket of his sweatshirt? In the back of his jeans? She knows, though, she is so distraught she could have missed a thousand clues.

"Did you carry that overseas?" asks Stu. "Mr. White has this huge collection of stuff he got off soldiers when he was in Japan, bayonets, little knives, a whole bunch of crap. But," he adds, "he doesn't carry them around. He just brings them to the garage sometimes to oil them up. Mrs. White complains about the grease at home."

"Nope. I got this here."

"Why?" Cassie asks.

"For protection. Here," he passes the gun over Cassie to Stu. It's clunky like a hammer, and the barrel dips down.

Stu holds up his hands. "No way, buddy," he says. "I don't want to kill someone by mistake."

"Like this?" Mark points the gun across the riverbank, aims into the darkness. "Pow," he whispers, "pow, pow, pow."

Cassie winces with each pow; there's something creepy and cold about the way Mark aims so carefully into the darkness.

"What the fuck?" says Stu. Sirens start nearby. "The cops are back, let's get out of here."

Mark turns to Cassie. "Run!" he commands. He pushes at her for emphasis, and she takes off down the alley and onto the sidewalk, moving in the orange shadows of the leaves below the streetlamps. The police, blue lights and sirens, careen down the street a few blocks down. Cassie dips into a threshold and then darts back toward the Pub, where the jukebox thumps its muffled bass of the out of the mouth of the open door.

Once inside, Cassie hesitates. A swarm of bodies separates her from where she sat with Teri and that Nina twenty minutes before. She is suddenly tired by the familiar crowd, by the smoky, gold-veined mirror over the bar. Will she ever be somewhere new?

Cassie finds Teri at the table where she left her.

"You look like you've seen a ghost," Teri remarks.

"In a way."

But she won't let go. "I didn't know you were still close to him, you didn't really talk about it."

Cassie doesn't know what to say. Are you close to someone because you think about him day and night? How could she explain how it felt to be with Mark, finally, close for a minute or two? "We wrote, back and forth. A lot."

Teri stares at her, chin down, eyebrows arched. "It's not over?"

Over? Everything feels over to Cassie, everything she

thought she understood. Teri would think she was crazy, doing it in an alley with a guy who has a gun, with Stu ten feet away. She wonders how long it will be before Teri gives up on her, before her choices become so alien that their friendship can no longer connect them.

Teri reaches her hand up and shifts the hair out of Cassie's eyes.

Nina is upon them. "We have to leave. I left a guy in the men's room who thinks I'm going home with him and I'm not." She pulls on Cassie's arm and moves toward the door. "Let's go, let's go," she hisses. With frequent backward glances, Nina works her way through the crowd.

They reach the outside, and a cooler breeze shifts the leaves. Nina looks down and laughs at her nipples, which point out of her thin halter. "Ooh, I'm chilly."

Teri snorts.

Cassie lifts her arm and waves. "See you," she says. "Call me," she adds, turning back to Teri.

That Nina is all offense and no defense, fumes Cassie. She walks by the alley that leads to the river, and she steals a glance sideward. Why wouldn't every guy want a girl like Nina, pretty and game for the world?

Cassie looks down the silent street, empty of passing traffic. Save a neon glow that spills onto the sidewalk outside the sub shop, the storefronts are dark shadows of wide glass, topped by smaller dark squares in the apartments above. Inside the only lit shop, a man in kitchen whites rubs a cloth over a table in brief circles, then goes on to the next one. Some relative of the Cosmos, more recently here from Greece, runs the shop. Cassie is unsure who exactly owns it. It is late, and there are no customers. That man certainly wasn't carrying a gun. What was Mark thinking he would need a gun for here? Was it a habit he had picked up? She remembers how angry he had gotten at the man at the gas station. "Did he have a gun then?" Would he have used it, or was he carrying it for some kind of protection or as a good luck charm?

Her father long asleep, she steps slowly through the darkened house before she creeps into her own room, shuts the door, and turns on the low lamp on the bedside table. On the bottom shelf sit Mark's letters, at least a year's worth, in a scattered pile. She hasn't thrown them out, but she hasn't looked at them more than once or twice; garrulous in print, he'd sometimes written so often that she'd just digest one before she'd receive another. At first, their frequency surprised her, but she'd soon gotten used to all the words, even loved them.

She pulls the envelopes out in a heap on her bed. Some are crumpled, dirty, or folded. None have a stamp, as soldiers overseas don't need stamps for the government to move their mail, but they are postmarked so that Cassie could sort them by date if she wanted. Most of them are in weightless, light blue envelopes, written on matching weightless stationery in small, neat handwriting. No loops, little slant, the sentences march across the page in even lines.

She picks up a letter off the top of the pile. "Dear Cass," it reads, "I had to hump my radio mucho clicks today." As he had learned the soldier's lingo, it became become familiar to her. He'd written her how he'd gotten radio duty because he'd shown an aptitude and how that had saved him from some of the more dangerous duties, like walking first on a patrol. She picked up another; this one starts: "You wouldn't believe how many layers I lost off the bottom of my feet since I've been gone."

When the letters had come, she'd read them in gulps, but perhaps the stories hadn't sunk in like they should have. He'd written a lot about his feet until the damp, the lost skin, and the sores became part of what she'd expected to hear. Now it shocks her to think about Mark's feet, the skin coming off in strips, in a way it hadn't shocked her at the time she'd learned of it. She hadn't even thought to ask him how they were now. She'd just assumed they'd be back to normal.

She picks up another letter and reads about a guy named Manuel who was shot on the perimeter of camp a few months back. His family had sent a letter to a squad member, begging for information, for stories about him, and no one had wanted to write back. Finally Mark had.

"What could I tell them?" he wrote.

"I'm afraid at night," he wrote.

"I want to come home," he wrote another time.

I can't stop what's running in my head, Mark had told her a few hours before. Cassie will never know exactly what's in his head, but a lot of it is also probably in these letters. He'd told her everything, but she hadn't listened. She had read them looking for the familiar, when it was the new information that she should have been paying attention to, that would have been clues to the changes to come. She shivers, worries that he already might be too far away from her to reach.

## June 21, 1971

The train out of Ipswich careens along the narrow rails that stretch across the pilings, which stick up from the water like the skeletons of a shaky pier. With a swerve to the right, the cars hit solid ground again and swoop through the concrete tunnel into Salem Station. As she stands, Cassie's palms slip on the leather seats in the stuffy car, already sweaty as she steps into the bright afternoon sunshine. She blinks and falls back from the burst of hot air that rushes by her as the train pulls away.

"The Locker Room," the ad in the phone book said, on Essex, off Washington just blocks from the train, but the station is set on the low end of the North River, with no main roads in sight. Broken glass flickers in the hardened yard dirt and, uncertain of her direction, Cassie follows the other stragglers from this off-hours train toward a steep, narrow metal staircase.

The top step brings her to a roar of traffic, exhaust fumes, and a rotary. Not sure whether Washington begins, ends, or merely dissects the rotary, Cassie considers asking the old man in the shade of his newsstand, but his loud complaints to a wide man in baggy pants bark over the traffic and send no sign of welcome.

Several blocks down, Cassie regrets her reticence to ask for help. The breezy ad in the yellow pages promised that the store was just down from the train station, but what if those were driving directions? Despite the quickening wind, the exhaust from a passing bus lingers, heavy and noxious.

Her canvas sneakers meet her ankles in the beginnings of a blister. Cassie chastises herself. Here she is, going almost into Boston, four towns down on the train line to find a special shoe store, and she didn't think to wear socks. A runner should take better care of her feet.

Once she finds Essex Street, bright red skinny letters on a white sign that swings above a broad, clean window advertise "The Locker Room." Across the air-conditioned threshold, the inside is all soft rugs and shiny metal shelves packed with different size rackets and golf clubs.

Running shoes, the ad called them, not sneakers, are either out of view or not available. Cassie closes her eyes and lets the cool air brush away the ticking of a small headache before she walks to the back of the store. A clerk bends into a large cardboard carton. "Excuse me," she begins, and he jumps up quickly, with an efficient swivel-and-stand motion, to face her. His hair is white-blond, his skin pink flushed on white, and he's as young as she is, but tall. "I'm looking for sn. . . running shoes."

He stares at her for the extra second needed to make her self-conscious, then nods. "All right," he says. "Whom would these be for?"

"Whom would these be for?"

"Who are they for?"

Cassie squints and tilts her head. "They would be for me."

His face turns the same startling color crimson as his neat polo shirt with stitched-on alligator on the left pocket. "Sorry. We don't get too many girls."

She shrugs.

He smiles at that and beckons with two fingers. She follows him through a blue-and-red–striped curtain hung on small rings into a cozy room lined with shoeboxes. "Sit," he says and points to a small stool. "Take off your shoes."

Cassie looks at her own worn sneakers and worries about

her feet, sweaty, swollen, and red after the walk from the train.

"Come on," he says, "they can't be worse than anything I've smelled before." He takes her damp foot and places it on the black metal measuring plate, lined in silver, with a small moving bar at the top. "You gotta wear socks, even if they're dirty, just turn them inside out," he admonishes her. "Like I said, we don't get many girls so we don't have much of a selection. I'm going to measure you for a man's foot too." He looks up at her. "You don't mind, do you?"

His eyes are clear, blue and straightforward. He pulls a brand-new pair of socks out of its packet and hands it to her, and then picks a shoebox off the shelf.

"Is there any difference?"

"Between the men's and the girl's shoes?"

"Yeah."

"Nah. Just the colors." As she puts on the thick, white socks, he threads the laces through the shoes. Head bent, his breath slow and even, he slips the shoes onto her feet, pulling the lace tight through each new set of eyes as he works his way up toward her ankles. He leans back. "How do they feel?"

She stands, lifts her knees up in turn, toes pointed down. The shoes, which sport a red stripe on either side, are lighter than anything she's ever worn.

"What's your distance?"

"Half mile's my best," Cassie answers him, forgetting that she hasn't run competitively in two years.

"Who do you run with?"

This question stops her short. She catches sight of the bright orange price tag on the shoebox, almost two days at Cosmo to pay for them, not including the socks or the train ticket.

*I run with no one because I go to a two-year school with no track team.* She sits back on the little stool. "My school, well, it doesn't really have track."

He sits on another little stool next to hers. "I know how it is, I have a sister. But, you know, some schools let girls run track now."

She nods.

"You like the shoes?"

She smiles at him. "Yeah, I like the shoes."

"They're the latest technology."

Cassie thinks of Stu, rebuilding his most recent car; I'm only using foreign parts this time, he claimed, only the latest technology.

"Who do you run with?" she asks.

"U Mass. I'm more of a distance guy. I want to do the marathon next spring." He holds out his hand. "I'm Rick, by the way."

She holds his hand, and they shake once. "Cassandra, but everyone calls me Cassie." Despite the cool air, she sweats as she reaches down to untie the shoes.

Rick watches her and then springs up to gather the box and its papers. "Keep the socks on before those blisters get worse." Her old shoes feel heavy and tight around the ankles, but the padded socks protect her skin.

Rick plucks a magazine from a stack by the cash register. "This issue's got a whole section on training," he tells her. "You know, what weights, what muscle groups." He curls the slick pages and slips them into the bright blue-and-red–striped plastic bag, along with the shoes and remaining socks from the packet he opened. She wants to track the cost of her purchases, but she suddenly can't remember the price of the shoes and doesn't want to ask the price of the socks or the magazine. She hands him all the bills in her wallet.

"Sometimes I like to go to Bradley Palmer for longer runs."

Cassie nods as he counts her money. She wonders whether she has enough to pay for her return train ticket.

He hands her the change. "You should let me know how it goes. Maybe we could run together sometime." Her head bent, she counts the change. Yes, enough for a ticket, she thinks, and then, did he just ask me out?

"That would be great," she says. I'm too out of shape now, she thinks, maybe I could come back after I've trained some more. She turns away from him, his white-blond hair mirrored a dozen times in the metal shelves behind.

Back on the sidewalk, the wind continues to increase, and to the east are the beginnings of heavy clouds. Cassie turns left instead of right and walks fifteen minutes to a neighborhood of sloping triple-deckers before she realizes she's gone in the wrong direction. She stops. None of the yards have grass and the nearest tree is two blocks down. Only the blue sky feels familiar. How can you stand all the square concrete buildings, all the noise, she'd asked Teri when she'd visited her at school. It's only for four years, Teri had answered, and then you can go where you want.

Has she missed the 3:41 that will bring her back to Ipswich in time for work? She turns and walks back. After ten minutes or so, she's back in the business block. Back by the Locker Room, she speeds up, head down so that Rick won't see her lost.

Traffic's increased at the rotary and from her vantage point high on the steps, Cassie sees the train coming in from the city as well as the crowd waiting at the station. She hurries down the stairs, across the yard, and into the car. This train's air conditioned, almost full, with most of the seats taken by men in shirts and ties. Cassie wonders if she's on the 4:10, which would make her close to late for work.

Maybe she could run by herself in Bradley Palmer Forest and she'd bump into Rick on some wooded path. Or maybe she could go to U Mass and be on the girl's track team and happen to see him at a meet. The train swoops out of the tunnel. By then, she'd be in shape and ready to run with him, or with anyone. But going to U Mass would mean leaving Ipswich. The train hits the piling bridge. She checks her sales slip. Rick had only charged her for the sneakers. The car sways to the left in an easterly wind and Cassie can feel the tracks shake on the bridge before the last car swerves to the right and the wheels hit solid ground.

Back in Ipswich, the heavy bank of clouds that hovers at the rim of the sky and the wind gathering speed over the water begin to feel like a nor'easter. The clock over the furniture store across the street from the station tells Cassie that the low tide is passed, and she must go directly to work without stopping at home to drop off her package.

Dark as it's growing outside, it's still several shades darker at Cosmo. Just as Cassie stows the bright blue-and-red–striped bag by the sink in the less frequented storage room next to the office, she is interrupted.

"It's just you and me today."

Cassie sidesteps toward the office.

David follows. "I'm going to bug out after the weighing, so…"

She shoves the bag under the desk as he idly shuffles a sheaf of papers.

"I want to be out of here at six, so I need your help."

"OK." She turns to the safe and kneels to work the combination.

"Um, Cassie?"

When Cassie turns the knob, she doesn't hear the usual click.

"Cassie?"

"George changed the numbers again."

He nods.

"Well?"

"Well?"

"Well, what are they?"

He won't look at her, and she watches his fingertips dance over the paperwork like spider legs.

"You can't tell me, can you?"

He shakes his head.

She rocks on her heels, hand on the safe for balance.

"But it's not you. It's just . . ."

She stands and glances toward the ceiling because he's watching her. When he's out of sight, she forgets just how handsome he is, all brown eyes and thick, curly dark hair.

"And, Cass, the checks arrived from the bank so we're going to write checks from now on. I thought that, ah, maybe you could do that part." He walks past her to the safe. She retreats to the door and looks to see if any clammers have arrived.

"Cass, look here." David holds a thick checkbook. "We have to record the numbers in all these different places and I . . ."

Cassie takes the checkbook, flips through the pages. Each check has a corresponding entry; she's seen this before, in a basic accounting class she took at community college. Plus, she thinks, it makes sense to keep track of who you give your money to. "You have to put the amount here," she points, "and then transfer it to the regular sheets."

"Sure," he answers, but he doesn't look at the papers.

"It's easy." She lays the sheets out on the desk. Her foot hits the end of the plastic shoe bag, and she kicks it farther under the desk.

"It's easy when you're good with numbers," David says.

She turns to laugh with him, but he's not smiling. He looks as grim as his grandfather in the picture behind him. This is not like finding a product and a market in a foreign country, she wants to tell him, this is the easy part. David waits, and she opens her mouth to answer just as a raucous hello sounds from the back of the building. She gathers the checkbook and papers into a neat pile. "Freddo's here."

"I'm not joking, Cass."

All right, she thinks, he's not joking, but anyone can learn this if he wants to. Maybe he doesn't want to. She smiles at him. "Let's go. I want to ask Freddo how his mother's doing."

He smiles back. "Freddo has a mother?"

David helps Freddo to pour his sacks of clams into the bushel baskets, and then he drags the weighed shellfish to where they'll be cleaned and put in the cooler to be sent on or shucked in the morning.

"What's it like out there?" David asks.

"White caps in the bay, wind from the east."

"Sounds like a nor'easter."

"Tomorrow's tide will be a loss," says Cassie, "and we're short for orders." She pulls over the stool, arranges her books on her lap, and writes Freddo out a check.

"What the fuck is this?" He waves the blue slip back and forth like a flag at David.

"Money, Freddo," says Cassie.

"Jesus, we're not getting paid?" someone yells from the back of the line.

"Hey," Cassie shouts. "You didn't hear? Someone came in here and stole a safe of cash, so now we're doing checks."

"All right, Cass," says Freddo. He folds the check three or four times before he puts it in his pocket. "And my mother says she wants to see that ring on your finger soon."

"No cash?" the same voice calls out.

"Shut the fuck up!" yells Freddo. "You heard what the lady said."

She smiles at Freddo.

Cassie and David work their way through the line; David weighs the clams and Cassie records the figures. It's fun, Cassie thinks, working together like this, and it might even be more efficient. The cash was bulky, awkward, while the numbers in their precise columns stay in one place and always mean the same thing. Even Andy Faragut pockets his check without too much complaining.

It's after six when they finish.

"Damn, my mother wants me home." David takes the stool and places it back near the freezer. "I don't want to go."

"I'll hose this down."

"You don't understand, Cass, what she's got planned for me."

She hesitates. David's got an open-eyed expression on his face that reminds her of Teri just as she's about to launch a long story about her parents.

"You just need to open the safe so I can put the books in." She heads for the office with David in tow.

"Come on, Cass." He opens the safe, but then lingers at the doorway.

What could his mother possibly have planned? "You can always tell her no."

"No?"

"Yeah, as in, no, I don't want to."

"You don't know my family."

Cassie thinks about this. Maybe he's right. She thought she knew about the Cosmos but maybe she doesn't. Maybe if David were born David Leahy instead of David Cosmo, the last job in the world he'd take was running his own shellfish company. Or maybe he wants to feel as if he has a choice. Teri insists everyone has a choice. She thinks of Mark, just as insistent, close to her. He'd asked her, what are you afraid of? She should turn that question on David. But he'd probably just say his mother, and Cassie doesn't want to hear that.

Big baby, she wants to tell him, big handsome baby, go home and tell your mother whatever you want. Your words won't send her away.

She turns around. He waits by the doorway. "It's only one night, David. I'll be here tomorrow and you can cry on my shoulder then."

The phone rings. "It's her! I've gotta go!"

But it's not Mrs. Cosmo. It's another restaurant chef in Boston, looking for mussels. "Not yet," she tells him. "We're not doing mussels yet."

"When?" the chef wants to know.

"Soon, we'll be doing them soon," she says, even though the only one at Cosmo Shellfish who wants to sell mussels is not even a Cosmo.

Outside, under a sky dark with angry purple clouds, the wind picks up, sweeping away what's light or not held down. As Cassie pedals home, newspapers, wrappers, a beach ball, maple seedlings blow by her, and the blue-and-red-striped bag swings along the handlebars.

Cassie wheels her bike to the overhang in the backyard. Oversized raindrops splatter the driveway. The kitchen bulbs glow neon in the lilac light of the storm, and Cassie stands outside a few moments as the rain quickens, trees snap overhead, and the lavender light shades to black. The wind pushes the rain at her, and she lets it run off her face and arms, like a cool shower.

Her dad shouts at her from the kitchen. "Cassie! There's something by the back steps you should bring in before the storm gets worse."

Cassie looks through the screen into the kitchen. What is it she wants to ask, but her father's over the stove, his back to her. He pops something sizzling into the fry pan so that she can barely hear the rain for the sound of the splatter. She looks over the side of the step. Pelted by rain sit two small wooden boxes, their tops and sides screened. She picks them up by their edges with her fingertips and holds them up to her face. Inside each are two or three large leaves. She turns each box around slowly until she spots the small white worms beneath the leaves.

Hard rain races across the steps and Cassie is soaked through. She brings the boxes into the kitchen and places them on the counter, away from the heat of the stove. Tiny, precise nails hold each corner, the screens at the top and sides are sandwiched between two slats of narrow wood, and the top piece slides off a track to open, like a tiny circus cage. She recognizes Mark's hand: no rough corners, no stray parts, neat and nice to look at. The creatures inside have plenty of air and light, and he gave them several days' food in case Cassie hadn't found them straight away. This is the work of the person who'd helped build boats with the bent-over old carpenter that worked behind the boatyard on the causeway, the one who'd made his mother window boxes three springs ago for Mother's Day. Cassie sniffs the freshly cut ends, notes the clean state of the nails against the wood. These were recently made. He hadn't left a note. He didn't need to.

"Looks like Christmas in June," says her father.

Cassie smiles as she puts her shoes next to the boxes. "I guess so."

"That boy always went in for that kind of thing."

"I guess he still does. You didn't see him?"

"Nope. They were on the steps when I came home. I can't see how I missed that bag, though. We could plug that thing in and use it as a table lamp."

"No, the bag's mine. I bought special sneakers. To run in."

"You always ran pretty fast in the ones you had."

"No, look at these." Cassie takes the sneakers out of their box. Amidst the faint scent of rubber, they look shiny and their red stripes shimmer. "They hardly weigh a thing."

Rain splatters the kitchen windows and comes in through the screen. Cassie shuts the back door with the heel of her foot.

"Is this what the girls are buying now?"

"No, they're really boys' shoes. They didn't have any ones for girls."

Frank Leahy turns back to his fry pan and gives the peppers, onions, and sausages a turn.

Cassie gathers plates, forks, and knives and two beers from the fridge and clears a spot for them at the table.

"I could have married to get you another mother, but I didn't want to do that. It never seemed right. But, I don't know." He puts a cutting board on the table with the fry pan on top and then brings out a bag of rolls.

Hungry, Cassie heaps the roll full. The last time she got this speech was at graduation. She had worn pants under her gown, while most of her friends had worn special summer dresses they'd bought with their moms. When the ceremony was over, and they'd taken off their gowns and spread out like flowers over the football field, she'd found her father deep in conversation with Mrs. Pinter. "I didn't know she'd need one," he'd said. "She only had to tell me."

"Look, Dad," Cassie says, "other girls run. The guy at the store told me all about it. There's even colleges that let girls run."

"They look like fancy shoes. Why don't you let me buy you the shoes?" He doesn't wait for an answer, but reaches into his back pocket, pulls out his wallet, and rolls out three ten dollar bills onto the table.

"Dad, you don't have to pay for the shoes."

"Why can't you let your father buy his only daughter a pair of shoes?"

She takes the money and puts it in her pocket because she knows he won't finish his supper until she does. "Thanks, Dad."

"You gotta find a man who can buy you a nice pair of shoes once in a while, OK?"

She reaches for a second roll.

"OK?" he repeats.

"Don't worry, I can take care of myself."

"It's a hard thing for a girl to take care of herself."

"I'm not just any girl."

"I know that."

"I'm your girl."

He snorts into his beer. "For now," but he slides all the stray peppers and onions into a sturdy pile on his plate before he scoops them into a fresh roll and Cassie knows that he's pleased.

The storm's rained out the ballgame, so Frank Leahy settles into the evening news while Cassie lays out her schoolbooks on the kitchen table. She is rereading the part where Nausicaa and her handmaids wash the royal laundry in the river. Odysseus shows up, naked, hair matted and long, one arm clutching a cluster of leaves for modesty, the other waving as he calls out to the washing party. The other girls scatter, but Nausicaa listens to his story, gives him something to wear, and takes him to her father, the king of the Phaeacians, who, like everyone else in the entire story, fails to recognize Odysseus. Cassie likes this bold girl and would like to include her in the essay she's composing for class, for Mr. Brooks.

Cassie watches the rain. Odysseus repeats his story, over and over again, to anyone who will listen, and no one ever recognizes him, even his own family. It's a wonder he doesn't just get tired of it all and stop trying to get home.

Cassie reaches into the blue-and-red–striped bag and pulls out the running magazine. A bronzed man with large calf muscles runs around a corner. Inside are ads for sneakers, special socks, even shorts. She turns to the section on weights that describes a weekly routine, done on a weight machine. Not just arms, but stomach, leg, and back muscle groups are covered. It's clear that this sophisticated weight program requires more than twenty-eight–ounce tomato cans. The only weight room Cassie has ever seen is in the high school and used exclusively by the football team. The building is open for summer school; what about the weight room? Cassie puts the magazine down. What was she thinking buying those sneakers? Will she run the soles bare doing circles alone around her high school track? She stands up.

In the living room, the news is still on, with President Nixon in front of microphones, promising once again to end the war once he's reelected. Cassie heads for her bedroom and takes out Mark's letters. On his way home, Odysseus lost his temper frequently and reached for his sword as often as he reached for food and drink at a feast, almost as if the relief of coming home were overshadowed by the experience of being away.

Cassie picks up from where she left off a few nights ago. But the rain against the windows makes her sleepy. She puts the papers down on the bed. She can't bear to go back and read about the cans of peaches in the middle of the night, the wet socks against the flayed skin, the lone leg in the boot, the body rolled over in the muddy puddle.

Cassie retreats again to the living room. Now it's helicopters on the TV.

Back in the kitchen, the running magazine waits next to her schoolbooks. In the backyard, the nor'easter is in full blow, and the pounding rain flattens the weeds. Cassie checks on the little white worms in their safe boxes and wonders how their cousins outside will weather the storm.

She remembers that night on the empty beach when they'd lain naked on the warm sand until almost dawn. The two of them had felt tiny and crowded by the world, and when he'd told her he didn't want to go, she'd felt lost and scared too: when his wet lips had pulled away from hers, the fraction of space between them had terrified her, as if a steel blade had sliced them apart, cutting her away from him forever. She'd pulled him back quickly, she remembers, and this had made him laugh. I'm not gone yet, he'd said to her. But, in a way, he was.

She'd looked over his shoulders at the rosy dawn turning a crest of the incoming waves pink and thought, I'm on my own now. She'd felt alone then, while he still held onto her, and in her heart, she'd left him to his fate. She hadn't tried to persuade him to stay, and then later she hadn't wanted to follow him into his nightmare, hadn't wanted to seal the words of his letters into her heart.

"Mark rescued you!" she whispers to the worms. "And your cousins are drowning!" But the insects don't respond, not even to move. It'll be a couple of days before they become green eating machines, and even then they'll pay her no attention.

She wants Mark, but calling doesn't seem right because she doesn't know what she would say. Neither of them was ever much for talking on the phone. Cassie puts the box down, puts her books away, and joins her father in the darkened living room, the walls flickering with the blue light of the TV.

### June 22, 1971

Rivulets, green with seedlings, stream down the driveway toward the backyard and the rain pounds ceaselessly against the east-facing kitchen windows. The winds have torn the petals off the early summer flowers, littering the hard surfaces with blotted wild colors, reds, pinks, blues, and yellows, like confetti. Cassie knows that down at the beach the gale is pounding its angry, salty waves into the parking lot, and that the causeway to Mark's house will be impassable.

Anxious to be out in it, Cassie waits by the back door with her books for her father to drive her to work.

The phone rings, its tones muted by the driving rain. It's Teri.

"Nina wanted to sun on the beach today."

This storm was rolling in by yesterday afternoon, Cassie thinks, but Teri has always ignored the weather. "Isn't Nina in Italy with her uncle?"

"Not yet, now she wants to go to work with my dad."

Frank Leahy stamps his boots on.

"Speaking of work, I gotta go, my dad's giving me a lift."

Teri sighs. "I wish I had your dad. He wouldn't be breathing down my back about squandering my potential."

Cassie glances at Frank, impatient at the doorway. He waits, in heavy boots and thick work pants, his shoulders wide from years of working with his arms and hands. A faded blue hooded jacket over his head shades his face. In this kitchen, he is her father, easily recognizable, distinct. In the crowd at quitting time, his lined, impassive face and blue work pants multiplied a hundred times, he could be anyone; to avoid mistakes when she picks her father up from work, Cassie waits for him to come to the car. The farther a person gets from home, the more like everyone else they become.

But now, in another second or two, he'll be out the door without her. "Things may clear up tomorrow, but it might still be windy," Cassie promises Teri.

"Teri wants you to be her father," she teases her dad as she hangs up.

He heads out the door. "Do I get a say in this?"

"I thought you liked Teri."

They dash to the car. "Egghead!" he shouts over the rat-a-tat-tatting of the raindrops thrown against the roof.

"What?"

"Egghead," he repeats. "Thinks too much."

Cassie smiles slightly, unsure of what her dad really means. Teri has always just done what she wants; Cassie worries that she's the one who thinks too much.

The streets are running with rain. The occasional person races by, hood up, jacket buttoned.

When Cassie gets out of the car at Cosmo, Frank hands her an umbrella. He turns from her and faces the rain streaming down the windshield. "Go on now," he barks. "You're letting all the rain in."

Even in the short steps from the car to the hut, Cassie is wet and, as soon as she steps into the air-conditioning, cold. She leaves her books in the storage room next to the office and pulls out a space heater. Slipping on her navy sweatshirt, she starts the coffee. George should be in, maybe even the old man whom she hasn't seen around much since the robbery. She wonders when the Cosmos will relent or forget and tell her the new combination to the safe. Most likely it'll be the next time they need her to fetch something out of it. The rain drones on the metal roof; nothing indoors, not even the forklift, makes as much noise in comparison.

There'll be no new clams this morning as the storm makes it impossible for the diggers to work, but the shucking must continue. They'll fill the priority orders, the regular customers first and then work on down to the little restaurants, which might not be having clams on their menu if the storm lasts more than four tides. Cassie goes to check out the shuckers' station.

Even though Cassie started at Cosmo as a shucker, she shares little camaraderie with this odd collection of part-time workers, all women down on their luck or women from Greece or Armenia who don't speak English, the latter group older, stooped and garbed in black like a pack of evil grand-mothers. They bring their own knives to slice through the resistant clam joints before dropping the slippery bodies into clean white buckets and discarding the shells. Cassie has learned that each woman's position at the shucking station defines one's place in a rigid pecking order; when she idly chose a spot on her first day of work a small, older woman wearing what looked like a collection of dark scarves bran-dished a knife in her face and started hissing in another language. After the others laughed, a worn blonde had ex-plained, that's Penuvia's station and she doesn't like to share.

Each of these older woman in black with thin gray hair pulled to a ball in the back of her neck reminds Cassie of the grandmother of a grade-school friend. In the middle of an after-school snack, the old woman would grab Cassie's wrist and intone in Armenian, her granddaughter patiently translating the woman's story of families forced out of their homes by the Turks, made to march for months, babies who died, mothers who collapsed from the weight of carrying their children. She ended each telling by spitting into the gleaming kitchen sink and cursing into eternity the souls of the Turks. The exact words of the curse varied with each ren-dition, but the vehemence with which the phlegm hit the sink, sixty years after the fact, stayed the same. The granddaughter, too, told the story in school, bound as she was, she explained, by her promise to her grandmother not to let the injustice go unforgotten.

Only a few clean white buckets are stacked near the shucker's stations, but when she checks outside the back door, Cassie spots dozens lying unwashed by the loading dock, the mud running in streams around them. She decides to wait for a letup in the rain to retrieve them and retreats to the office where the coffee perks and the daily runs await organization. If David hadn't needed help with the checkbook yesterday, these runs would be done. She looks at the clock; Dodie and Paul will be here any minute to load up the trucks. Maybe she should have stayed to do them last night.

Cassie sits at the desk, collects the separate order sheets into a neat pile, and divides them into three separate delivery runs. She then tallies the buckets of soft bellies, full clams, or scallops needed by each vendor, makes out a delivery sheet, and keeps a running tally for loading.

George, his face tan from his weekend on his boat, steps into the small office holding an oversize wrench.

"If you got a new freezer," Cassie says, "you'd save the time you spend fixing it, you'd be able to keep the fish in there longer, and you might save on electricity."

"Why are you doing those now?" he asks her as she hands him a cup of coffee.

She sits back down. "Dodie's sheet is done, Paul's is almost, and who's the third driver?"

"David's the third driver today. Poli quit. We'll get someone else in a day or two."

The Greek network infiltrates the North Shore, and George has an unending supply of relatives who are looking for a job.

"Why didn't you do these yesterday?"

"David needed help with the checkbook," she answers, not

looking up. Light House Restaurant, didn't she already do this order? She shifts through the sheets until she finds it. George stays in the doorway, wrench in hand, sipping his coffee while he watches her work.

"Cassie," he finally says. "When are you finished with school?"

"Soon."

"How is that boyfriend of yours?"

What boyfriend she almost answers, but she knows he means Mark. "Fine."

"You know the stories. Some of them come back, you know," he swings his wrench around his head, "crazy, wild, bad."

"Mark's not bad," she says.

"Good." George shifts his weight uneasily and places his cup on the desk. "Cassie . . ."

He is interrupted by Paul's mournful voice. "Well, I'm here."

"You're not driving fish today," says George, his round face instantly cheerful at Paul's melancholy demeanor, "you're driving monkeys!"

Cassie smiles uneasily. Paul looks to heaven for assistance. Dodie arrives next to his cousin, his white hair a shock in the grey office. "We're driving monkeys today," reports Paul.

"Are they wearing diapers?"

Cassie laughs and so does George.

"I'm sure they're not," says Paul.

Cassie hands the cousins their papers. They leave to load the trucks.

David appears. "Yours will be ready in a minute," says Cassie. "Why don't you . . . " and she stops herself from telling him to go load the trucks with Paul and Dodie in front of his father.

David leans against the doorway and yawns. "It's nice and warm in here."

George asks, "Is the station set up?"

"We need more buckets," says Cassie.

"Go get some buckets," George says to his son. "Cassie will bring you the sheets." When David disappears into the gloom, George asks, "Do you still have those brochures about freezers?"

Cassie stops herself from smiling. "Sure I do, somewhere around here."

He puts down the coffee. "When you're done with that, why don't you try and find them."

"What are you smiling about?"

Cassie starts and looks up. David replaces his father in the doorway.

"I hope it's me." He's as dry as a bone so she guesses he hasn't gone after the shuckers' buckets.

Nervous under his full attention, she answers primly, "I was smiling about freezers."

"All work and no play makes Cassie a dull girl."

She hands him his papers. "Nothing I can do about that."

George reappears. "Let's load up the truck!"

Cassie gets up to file the extra delivery and load sheets until tomorrow's run.

With a start she remembers how, in the alley by the river, Mark had taken her by surprise, the rough way he'd pushed her back against the warm bricks of the building and how she'd responded, completely and without thinking. Now, the thought of what she'd allowed to happen, what she'd done, surprises her again.

The papers she holds quiver, and she rubs her hands on her jeans to stop their shaking, but it's of no use. It's not the cold that makes her shake. It was what she thought she wanted. In fact, the small office has gotten hot. She shuts off the space heater before she sits back at the desk to look for the freezer unit brochures she'd collected in the early spring, when Cosmo was gearing up for the season and both freezers crossed over from cranky to unreliable.

After a few minutes she finds the brochures, shiny and stiff and upbeat, in the large bottom drawer, tucked between the maintenance logs for the trucks. She'd written the prices in pen on the margins of the brochures, but at this time of the year, well into the season, perhaps they could get some kind of break. Or the dealer, sensing a disaster, might also raise the price. She'd have to let George make the call—no dealer would bargain with her, with her girl's voice and her undefined position—but only after she'd pointed out to him what prices she'd been quoted in March.

George doesn't like to be nagged, so she'll just leave the brochures out in full view. She won't even have to tell him they're there. To clear a space on the desk so that they'll be seen easily, she picks up the stray papers and, glancing over them, discovers a section of delivery sheets for David's run. In her rush this morning, she hadn't stapled the whole pile together. She jumps up. He'll never check the papers she gave him; David won't realize he has only half the route until he's halfway done the route.

Once she leaves the confines of the office, the pounding rain on the roof is deafening so that she is both aware of the protection the roof offers and the dangerous force of the water. Papers in hand, she heads toward the bays. Although the area is wet, the doors are closed. David hadn't time to load the truck himself, so Dodie and Paul must have helped him. If the trucks have gone, she's too late, but with the noise of the rain the three of them could be yelling to each other just outside the delivery bays and Cassie wouldn't hear.

She runs to the back door and opens it a crack. Rain runs off the lip of the roof like a curtain. A blur of red taillights turns out of sight, but another truck idles in the lot. She tucks the papers under her sweatshirt with one hand, pulls up the hood with the other, and shoulders her way out the door and into the rain.

The yard is alive with running streams and mud and rain

and Cassie is soaked when she reaches the idling truck and bangs at the side of the passenger door. She can barely hear her own knocking over the rain, which pounds on the metal roof of the cab with the same callous insistence it pours over everything open to the sky. With a quickly dismissed thought of what would happen if the truck pulled out suddenly, she puts her foot on the runner and lifts herself up by the door handle in order to pound on the window. Although the rain makes streams down the glass, Cassie sees David in the driver's seat, so she knocks again.

He leans across the cab to unlock the door for her. She's nearly thrown off into the mud as the door opens while she's still on the runner, but she manages to shift around the other side of the door while David grabs her arms and pulls her into the cab. Water streams over her skin. As he shuts the door behind her, the wide-open sense of water and sound contracts to the drumming of the rain on the cab roof.

She shivers, a quick hunch of the shoulders, and he rubs his hands up and down her arms, pulls her toward him, and kisses her, insistent, charging forward as if she weren't there. His hands move to her back as their two bodies slide down against the double seat of the cab. Yes, she thinks in a flash, this is fun too, like being on a roller coaster or swung too long against one's will on a playground tilt-a-whirl.

But there's nothing familiar about him. He's all urgency, and she understands completely that this is how it happens, this is how the girl gets into trouble, and this is the kind of guy.

She shakes her head.

"Come on, baby," he whispers, as much as a person can whisper with pounding rain on a metal roof inches from one's head, "you know you like it."

She feels sure he wouldn't say that to her if she were a Greek girl, with an entire Greek family waiting for her at home. She pulls her hands up in front of her and pushes hard against his chest. He makes a moaning sort of noise, and she pushes again and sits up.

He kisses her hair. "Cassie," he says, "I thought you'd never let me in."

But I haven't, she wants to say. Along with her quickened breath, wet clothes, the thrill of him here wanting her, is the ceaseless rain like a drum sounding danger in a monster movie. She can't ignore the waves of mistrust running through her. She reaches under her sweatshirt and pulls out a bundle of soggy, crumpled papers. "You forgot your delivery sheets."

"That's boring, Cassie," he singsongs and reaches his long fingers behind her back.

She moves toward her side of the truck. "Not here," she says. He moves toward her; she puts him off, kisses him lightly. "I have to go. Your father."

The air in the cab feels sodden and chilly. He loosens his hold on her and sits back. "My mother's the problem."

She places the wet papers on the seat between them. Now that David is safely defused, she doesn't blame him, feels sorry for him almost. "It's all right."

"You don't understand."

But she's cold, and she wonders if anyone has noticed her absence. "Your dad," she reminds him. At this, David stares at the raindrops splattering the broad windshield and hood of the truck. Cassie opens the door, jumps out, and shuts the door quickly.

She makes her way back across the yard. The wind is behind her and she's pushed along, almost over, her feet slipping in the shifting mud. By the loading dock, she detours to collect a pile of buckets. She tries to stack them, but the wide wet plastic sides slip through her soggy sweatshirt arms, jamming her fingertips between the metal handles and the bucket. She returns for another two or three loads and then drags the lot inside. By now, she is drenched.

The hut, always air conditioned, is raw and cold and Cassie's hands ache. She grabs the buckets by their handles, careful to keep her fingers free and brings them in groups to the hoses where she washes them off before delivering them to the women at the shucking station. The black-garbed figures are quiet as the rain storms the roof, and the clams fall rapidly and noiselessly into the buckets.

The handle of the rogue freezer is loose again, so Cassie makes sure to open it steadily. Inside, her chill turns to frost and she shivers as she lugs two full bushels of clams over to the shuckers. When they're out of clams, they'll have to move to scallops. Her cold, wet clothes sting her skin as she moves, and her shivers threaten to turn into the shakes. She walks as quickly as she can back to the office, thinking only of the space heater.

Old man Cosmo sits at the desk. His round shoulders roll forward, and the skin droops gently off his balding head in neat wrinkles. He looks tanned and handsome in his blue work shirt, and what hair he has is white and showy. "Cassie," he greets her, "you should take better care of yourself."

As best she can, she pulls the sodden sweatshirt off her shoulders and arms and over her head and crouches down in front of the heater. "David forgot half his delivery sheets," she starts, "and then the shuckers were about to run out of buckets." The heat warms her skin. If she leans into the heater long enough her shirt might dry out, but her jeans will remain soaked and heavy for hours to come. She glances up at the black-and-white photo of the old man in his youth, broad shouldered and squat, squinting into the sun, fingers curled into his fists.

"You work this place like you own it," says the old man. "That's what I told that cop. Not Cassie, I told him."

"You need better locks. The one in front is loose." Cassie twists her hair tight, and water falls in a puddle to the floor. "Maybe you could lock the office because whoever did it will probably try it again."

"That's what I told George."

"He just wanted quick money."

"Bah. Quick money is gone quick."

Cassie smiles up at the old man. She's missed him. He's been around so little, he seems half into retirement. Most likely, with David's full-time arrival, Cosmo will continue to do less. Cassie's eyes sting; the heater dries out her face, and she stands to distance herself from it. Her wet pants hang heavy against her legs. She may have to save time to go home to change before today's class. She ponders George's questions about her boyfriend; does he think that Mark had something to do with the robbery? His voice interrupts her thoughts.

"Uncle!" George holds the freezer brochures. "Here, look at this." He lays the brochures on the desk like a fan.

"When were these prices quoted?" the old man asks.

"In March," Cassie answers.

George glances at her. "What happened to you?"

"She got wet," says old man Cosmo.

"What were you doing? You're gonna catch pneumonia."

"No I'm not," but she shivers.

The old man gets up. "She needs a cup of coffee." He pours coffee into a thick, chipped mug decorated with a faded blue-and-white Greek flag and mixes in several spoons of Cremora. "Sit."

Cassie takes the cup and sits facing the heater. The coffee's hot and little lumps of unstirred Cremora float along the top.

"You sit here and see what this afternoon and tomorrow look like. Maybe make a few calls, see who can get by with less."

Cassie nods. "I have to leave for class at ten thirty, but I can come back after if you want."

"No," says George.

"Cassie," says Cosmo, "you're too pretty to be working in a fish house."

"If we had mussels coming from up north, that would be another buffer against the storms."

George shakes his head. "Most storms move along the whole coast."

"I'm too old for mussels." Cosmo ends the discussion. He taps the desk. "But not for a new freezer.

"You take care of the deliveries, Cassie," says George. "That's enough for today."

George disappears. Cassie dips her nose into the coffee cup to let the steam warm her face. Cosmo picks up a rain jacket from a hook and places a black cap with a braided brim on his head. He looks almost jaunty. "You young people," he says, "you've got to think about your future. My daughters, they both married nice, right out of school. This fish business, it's irregular. You don't want hard, Cassie."

She looks up at the old man and smiles. "I could go for warm right now."

He nods at her and leaves.

The wet fabric of her pants' leg brushes over her calf as she twists to reach the regular orders file. The rain will drive away customers too, so they will all get by on less for a few days. She's made these calls before, will easily negotiate temporary diminished deliveries and readjust the daily tallies. Too pretty to work in a fish house, what was the old man talking about? Cassie's done everything at Cosmo but drive the trucks. What has she been for the last four years—not pretty? She certainly has been working.

At ten thirty, the rain's hollow echoes still fill the Quonset hut. Outside, the wind reverses her umbrella before she leaves the Cosmo lot, and Cassie quickly decides that by the time she walked home to get dry pants and then walked back to the train station, her clothes would be wet again.

As the train station lacks both bench and cover, Cassie waits in the phone booth near the furniture store. Damp, cramped, with the rain pulsing against one side of the glass and leaving weary trails of its downward trip on the other, she perches on the little bench and feels sorry for herself. After a few minutes the booth fogs over and she can no longer see out.

Did George see another one of those news stories about a soldier who comes home a heroin addict and does all kinds of crazy stuff only to disappear again and then decide that Mark robbed the safe? Mark's not like that, even though, Cassie hesitates, he has gotten kind of wild and impulsive in a scary way. He didn't need to come up on her in an alley, for example; she's been wanting to feel his body for over a year. He was almost like David in that, in a creepy way. She thinks of David. Would she even think of him at all if it weren't for his shellfish company? Even if he did care for her, which seems unlikely because mostly David cares about himself, he would never seriously consider an outsider.

Still, Mark would never sit down and decide to steal money, she is sure of that. If Mark weren't so unpredictable she could bring him to work and let George see that for himself. Cassie shivers and rubs her hands together. Her fingertips are pruned and moist. With luck, the conductor will have thought to turn off the air-conditioning in the cars.

She feels the rumbling of the coming train, and a minute later it pulls up behind the furniture building and opens its doors.

The car is not cold at all, but steamy with heat and almost empty. The windows are fogged with a thick curtain of moisture and instead of cold, she feels wet all over.

At the other end of the ride, ankle-deep puddles, a wind tunnel, and slick granite steps make the walk to class feel more treacherous than usual.

Inside, the dry old building seems to absorb the wet bodies, with a light fog that rises above the stairwell. The chill, though, has set in her, and when Cassie finally reaches the classroom, her skin is covered in goose bumps.

Mr. Brooks arrives wearing long yellow fisherman's boots and a long yellow slicker, which he hangs on a hook behind the door. Underneath, he is nearly dry. Even his briefcase, wrapped in thick plastic, emerges with only a few dark droplets. He touches the sides of his head with the tips of his fingers to brush back some wet hair and checks his chair for dampness before he sits down.

"Chrono—time. Chronological order, to organize events by time, time in a straight line."

Cassie looks around. The class is smaller than usual, and Angie isn't here.

"Who can list in chronological order where Odysseus has been since he left Troy?"

Craig Murphy shuffles through his *Western Literature*. Doesn't he start out on the island?"

Mr. Brooks runs the tops of his fingers along the desk.

"That's where we first meet him," says Cassie.

"Ah hah!" shouts Mr. Brooks. The rain still beats against the large windows and the wind rattles the old glass, but Mr. Brooks' shout manages to make most of the students jerk up in their seats.

Cassie goes on, although reluctantly because Angie was the one who had already pointed this out. "The first place he went after Troy was that little city he massacred."

Craig Murphy looks up from his book. "He tells us where he's been, starting in Book IX."

Mr. Brooks stands up and writes on the chalkboard the different places Odysseus has been as the students call them out—with the Phaeacians, Circe's Isle, the Cyclops, the descent into Hades, to Calypso. This is not as easy as it first seems. Mr. Brooks must erase and rearrange almost every other time he writes a word. Sometimes Odysseus tells us where he's been and sometimes the narrator does, and this information does not come in order.

"Look," says Mr. Brooks after the list covers the board in his precise lettering, "Book I begins with the gods, next we move to Ithaca, Odysseus' home. Odysseus himself only appears partway through to tell some fantastic tales and then the narrator picks up again and relates his final journey home. Where he has been and what he has done is something we must put together ourselves. And what are we to make of Odysseus' stories? Are they relevant to the listeners at home? Look at this crazy jazz," and he points to the board. "He got captured by a witch? His men were turned into pigs? A one-eyed giant wanted him for dinner? He went to hell and saw all his buddies?" Mr. Brooks turns to the class. "You believe all this?"

The rain blasts against the windows.

"But, Mr. Brooks, all those gods and Athena popping up everywhere, it's crazy."

"You think the dinner guests believed all those wild stories? Or were they humoring a man who fought their enemies so they could stay at home?"

Bill starts to laugh from the back of the classroom. "Mr. Brooks, you are the true man of many wiles."

"Point of view," answers Mr. Brooks. "Look at who's telling the story before you listen to their words." He sits back down and touches the hair at the sides of his head again with his fingertips. "Their lying words."


This time Mark waits for her just inside the threshold. As she hesitates with the other students at the front door open to the storm, he grabs her arm and pulls her forward, out of the crowd. He is wet through, without greetings and urgent, wearing jeans and a maroon sweatshirt she's never seen before.

"Let's go," he says in an undertone, glancing at the crowd. He takes her arm and moves out the door, and the students step aside for them, as if something heavy were pushing from behind. He runs lightly and quickly down the steps, glancing from side to side, so that Cassie finds herself looking around too, and this puts her on the alert. Trailing her umbrella, her heart races as they cross the yard, straight through deep gullies of rain, to his car, still running, parked illegally across a service driveway.

Inside the heater's been blasting for a while. "Ahh," he says, "feels like my home away from home," and Cassie knows he's talking about the wet and the heat, that this is what it was like in the jungle.

She remembers a news story that aired in the winter. Some girl, to welcome home a soldier, had woven messages in flowers into the chain-link fences of a dozen overpasses, so that the returning soldier could read them as he passed under from the airport to his home. Why hadn't she done something like that?

She lifts her sodden feet closer to the heater. "As long as our toes don't rot off."

He laughs. "That would stink. But," he adds as he checks a full three hundred and sixty degrees around before he pulls away from the curb, "that would be kind of familiar too."

He grips the wheel as she leans across him to wipe the inside of the windshield with her sodden sleeve, cutting a clear swath in the fog. "You can relax now, you've got dry socks at home."

"No," he says, "I can't relax."

Rain streams down the windshield; she still can't see anything for the blur. She reaches over and flips on the windshield wipers.

"Oh Jesus," he says, "see what I mean?"

The speedometer barely reads twenty. As Mark drives he shifts his head from side to side, as if looking out the front window were not cautious enough. At least he's not speeding like before, Cassie says to herself. To be moving so slowly is a little strange, but doesn't feel dangerous. His mood seems to match the storm, all motion and alarm. And, although beer bottles still roll around under the seats, she doesn't smell any signs of his drinking. They must be old bottles. She wonders, though, what he's done with that gun and whether it was ever loaded.

She's still soggy, but there's too much heat in the car for her to be cold. She leans back against the seat and a sigh moves out of her, and she tilts her head to the side and opens her eyes a crack to peek at him. Mark leans forward into the rain, his hands tight around the wheel, all concentration and focus. Although leaner than when he first left her, his arms are wide and strong looking, although his hair's a little longer and his face still looks thin and very tired. His eyes, too, seem harder, but then she's hardly looked him full in the face since he came home. Cassie thinks about how all the students got out of his way when they left the building and made their way down the steps.

"Where did you find those white eggs you left me?"

His arches his neck forward so that it almost touches the steering wheel and then pulls it back. "In your backyard," he says, several moments later.

Out the window, the rain slackens. "I like the little cages."

He doesn't stop in front of the house, but pulls into the driveway. Newly ripped leaves still blow down the sidewalk, but the rain has slowed, the drops are smaller, and the light less gray, more yellow. As Cassie reaches into the back to grab her bag, his eyes dart over her the way the sun flashes on the surface of moving water.

"You wanna come in?" she asks.

He turns the car off and follows her into the dim, somewhat chilly kitchen. Cassie moves to turn on the heat but Mark hesitates, almost swaying, by the back door, all his previous energy dissipated, suddenly turned off. He looks exhausted, his hair pasted flat against his skull, his skin gray and drawn down over his cheekbones as if he hasn't slept in weeks. Water drips off the sleeves of his maroon sweatshirt onto the floor.

"Sit down," she says, "I'll make some soup." He slides onto a chair while Cassie checks through the shelves to locate a couple of cans of chicken noodle soup, a can opener, and a clean pan. She leaves these on the counter next to the box of her still-untouched running shoes, goes to her bedroom, and shuts the door. As quickly as she can, she strips off her layers of sodden, heavy clothing and pulls whatever is clean and dry from her dresser. Her skin is pickled and raises goose bumps before she covers it with a dry sweatshirt and jeans. She then goes into her father's room, pulls out a clean shirt and socks, and brings them back to the kitchen. Mark has opened the soup, put it on the stove, and stands by it, stirring slowly while he stands in an increasing pool of water on the linoleum.

"Here." She hands him the dry clothes. He takes off his sweatshirt and the shirt underneath and stands briefly naked from the waist up. She watches him twist into the shirt and, as he does, she catches sight of a bright red mark on his stomach. "Wait," she says and lifts up his shirt. Just below his rib cage, on the left side, is a thin, bright red scar about four inches long. It looks as if someone sliced him with a knife. Her first urge is to bend over and kiss the wet, raw skin, but Mark stands tense, as if he barely tolerates her scrutiny. She runs her fingers along the red crease and then places the shirt over it.

He turns from her. "Why," she says to his back, "would you tell me everything there is to know about foot fungus and not mention that?"

He shrugs, inscrutable, sits, and pulls a bowl of soup toward him.

They eat across from each other. Cassie's hungry and the warm soup makes her realize just how cold she was.

"Mark," she says and he looks up quickly. "Someone stole a lot of money from the Cosmos last week." His eyes aren't focused. He shuts them and shakes his head.

"Oh yeah?"

"Yeah."

"That prick still work there?"

"What prick?"

He yawns. "Mr. Basketballhead."

"David?"

"That's the one, David Basketballhead." Mark leans forward, his arms hunched over the table.

"What's wrong with him?"

"He's a pussy."

"How can you be a prick and a pussy at the same time?"

He smiles and closes his eyes, a million miles away. "It's possible."

Cassie stands, stacks their bowls, and puts them in the sink. She looks out at the yellow sky, the wet weeds.

"I can't sleep at night," he says.

She turns and looks at him, slumped at his chair. "Does everyone come home feeling like this?"

"How the fuck should I know?"

But he is more tired than angry, not like when he turned on her for asking about the guys on his patrol. Although most of them came and went, a few of them had been there for most of Mark's tour, had been there at the end, until he had said that there was no one left. She remembers the names, Lenny, Blipboy, Tarbox.

She proceeds carefully. "What about someone who came home before you, like Lenny maybe ..."

"Lenny came home before me all right. He came home in pieces." Cassie winces at his description. The flat way he reports this is more frightening to Cassie than his anger. It reminds her of how he mocked pulling the trigger of his gun aimed into the darkness across the river. This is new, this ability to experience the most horrifying events with a bland numbness.

"I'm really sorry." Cassie stops. Maybe, she thinks, I can do this a little bit at a time. So far, Mark hasn't exploded. "He was the one from North Dakota, wasn't he? The one you were going to visit when you got home?" She doesn't add that Mark had wanted to take her with him, to visit this magical place Lenny went on and on about.

He stares out the window, and she is not sure that he's listening. "This makes me crazy. I should just leave." His head slips to the side, almost pulling his body along, as if he could fall off the chair onto the damp floor, dead asleep. "I should leave everyone in peace."

"What's that supposed to mean?"

"What good am I? I can't even sleep right." He yawns.

"You look like you could sleep now."

"Look, Cass, I ..."

"Why don't you try?"

She pulls at his arm, and he follows her into her bedroom. They sit down on the bed. "I saved all your letters," she tells him.

He stares at the pile under her nightstand. "In case I didn't come back?"

"No!"

"You don't have to do this," he says as he starts to stand.

She pulls him back. "Mark, if you want to sleep, just sleep." She looks at her pruned toes on the floor while he takes off his pants and climbs under her sheets.

He rolls onto his side, speaks into the pillow. "I can't sleep in my parents' house anymore."

She nods.

"I'm going to have to leave," he says again.

She waits on the edge of the bed. In less than a minute, she hears him breathing slowly, heavily. It seems sad to her that this is the first time he's ever slept in her bed.

The kitchen reflects the pale, yellowish light that breaks through the storm. Cassie turns on the faucet, washes the pan, the spoons, the bowls, dries them, and returns them to the shelves.

She places her schoolbooks on the table. How could anyone go away for twenty years and expect things to be the same when he comes back? How could *The Odyssey* possibly have a happy ending? Cassie flips idly through the remaining unread pages. When will they meet Penelope, the wife who waited? Mr. Brooks has already told them that Penelope spends her days weaving and her nights undoing what work she's done during the day. So, after twenty years, she has nothing to show but some worn-out thread?

Cassie shuts the book, checks the clock. Her father will be home soon. Maybe she should move Mark's car out of the driveway to make room.

Outside, the pavement is wet but the air is warmer and the sun glistens on the wet leaves, making them look clean and new. The keys sit in the ignition, where he always used to leave them. Some things haven't changed.

The car interior is steamy and damp and filled with trash. She retrieves a trash bag from the kitchen. Mostly it's beer bottles and stray papers, but the ashtray has a few roaches. People who watch the news, people like George Cosmo, probably think every returning vet is some hopped-up drug maniac, but Mark smoked some before he left. Cassie never did; it was too harsh when she tried it, but mostly she didn't want to mess with her lungs and lower her race times. A haze of ashes rises up from the ashtray when she dumps its contents into the trash bag. Cassie leans back out of the way, balancing her foot up against the dashboard. The glove compartment shifts in its socket. She puts her foot down, hesitates, and then pulls it open. Inside rests an ice scraper, the current registration, a handful of old registrations, and, tucked at the back end of the well, a gun.

At first, Cassie is afraid to touch it. But here in front of her is the thing that Mark apparently got so attached to that he can't stand to be without one now. She curves her pointer finger into the loop of the trigger and draws it out. Nuzzle down, she holds it in front of her face. It smells oily, like some of the car parts Stu has strewn around his backyard.

She wonders if it's the same one Mark had down by the river, or if he's on his way to owning an arsenal. She wonders if it's loaded. Bullets or not, it's probably against the law to carry a gun around in your glove compartment. Against the law or not, it seems the action of a person screaming for trouble to come and find him. She gently places the gun back into its hiding spot, covering it with the papers and the ice scraper. How is she going to ask him about this? She shifts to the driver's seat, moves the car to the front of the house, and heads back inside.

As she passes by the backyard, Cassie stops by the patch of damp weeds. She leans over a sturdy, foot-high plant, and rips off a thick leaf. Milky beads form at each end of the wound. She shakes off the rainwater and transports the fresh leaf back inside and into one of the wooden cages Mark has made. She is moving the cage into a patch of sun on the counter when someone, Mark, shouts, hoarse and guttural.

In her bedroom, Mark shifts back and forth on the bed. Cassie steps toward him, and for a split second, with his eyes still closed, he sits up and flails his arms. The back of his hand catches her just below her left eye and sends her backward onto the floor.

He falls back to the bed, his breathing returns to slow and heavy. Cassie sits up, leans against the wall. Cautiously, she stands, peers over her bed. Mark is back on his side, sleeping. He doesn't know what he's done.

Her left eye and cheek burn with pain. She extracts ice cubes from a frosty tray in the freezer, dumps them into a dish towel, and holds the cold mass over her left eye and cheek. Her skin stings and pulses at the point of impact.

When Frank Leahy comes home, he finds her sitting at the kitchen table, staring at the yellow curtains, a dish towel full of ice on her face. His smile hardens as quickly as water in January.

"The hell happened to you?"

Cassie sits up quickly. She hadn't expected his anger.

"It's OK, Dad," she starts.

"Like hell!" He walks over to her and pulls her arm back. "Jesus Christ, someone belted you!"

"It was an accident! Mark . . ."

He paces quickly around the kitchen, looks at the back door. "Where is he?" He whips toward the living room. "I saw his car parked out front."

Cassie stands and moves in front of him. "Daddy!" she says and holds his arm.

Impatient, he shifts away from her, but he stops.

"Mark picked me up from class, because of the rain. He was so tired he could hardly walk and I told him to take a nap . . ."

He starts to move away and she grabs his arm back.

"He had some kind of nightmare, and I went in there and his arms were flying and I, I got hit. By him. But he doesn't know it." The impulse to cry and have her dad hold her pops up, but she pushes it away because her dad is upset enough already.

Now Frank looks at his daughter. "He doesn't know he hit you?"

"No, he did it in his sleep. And he hasn't woken up." She lets her father go and sits back down at the table. "He's kind of a mess, to tell the truth, Dad. He's like himself, but not himself, like he's been all shaken up. And," she stops before she tells him about the scar on his stomach or the gun in the glove compartment.

"And?" he prompts her.

"And his parents don't see it."

Frank Leahy snorts. "That doesn't surprise me." He goes to the fridge for a beer and then sits down at the table next to Cassie. He cups her face in his hands and gently presses her cheekbones and around her eye. She winces slightly. "Nothing's broken," he says and leans back. "The ice was a good start, but you're gonna have a shiner, that's for sure." He pops off the top and drinks. "Your head feel OK?"

"Yup."

"You dizzy or anything?"

She shakes her head.

He rubs his hands over the top of her head, like he used to do all the time when she was small. "The Leahys are tough," he says. "Sometimes too tough."

He sits back in his chair and stares at her a few minutes. "You sure you're OK?"

She nods.

"Mark must be sleeping like the dead to snore through all this commotion."

She laughs, relieved, but then she remembers Mark slumped over his soup at the kitchen table. "He says he can't sleep at home."

"Well, we're not running a motel."

"No, I know that, Dad. It's just that, he looked so tired."

"Yeah, I know." He finishes his beer, plunks it hard on the table. "Hungry?"

She nods. She is hungry.

"How about we go get some food?"

She smiles. "But what about . . ."

"We'll let him sleep."

"But . . ."

"Cassie, you need to take care of yourself."

Cassie nods again. This is the second time today someone has told her she needs to take care of herself. *I'm trying,* she thinks.

They drive down to the wharf and park in the lot that slopes down toward the river, the one that's crammed with the trailers of recreational boaters on the weekends and, as the river mouth has just a few moorings, less busy with lobster and small fishing boats during the week. Hettie's is a slanting house on the banks, the paint in dark green shreds on wide clapboards and a small yard in the back, on the river.

Inside, the ceiling's low and the smell of grease hangs heavy in the air. The sun glints and sparkles on the brown water through the row of windows that look over the bank.

"Frank!" calls out a large woman in a shapeless blue dress, gray hair wrapped like a funnel over her head. "You got Cassie!" She peers over the counter. "Sweetheart! What happened to you?"

"A freezer at work, Mrs. Cotter," she lies quickly.

"Mm mm," Hettie Cotter answers, disbelief all over her face. "I hope that freezer keeps his hands to himself next time."

"You got clams?" asks Frank Leahy.

Hettie Cotter's little place on the river is not on the Cosmo delivery route. "I'm open, aren't I?" she snaps.

"Let's get a large order then, with some slaw and fries," he says, "and we'll take them outside."

The miniature yard is protected from the wind, with crabgrass and two picnic tables painted the same color as the house covered in a clear, oily plastic. The brown river flows quiet a few feet beyond.

They sit.

"She didn't believe that freezer story for a second," laughs Frank Leahy. "She probably thinks I did it."

Cassie laughs. "I don't think so."

Frank produces another beer from his pocket and pops open the top. The sky is moving, with a shrinking mass of storm clouds to the east and a growing clear blue to the west.

When they arrive, the clams are hot and crunchy on the outside, their bellies warm and liquid on the inside, the ketchup sweet and the slaw cold. An icy Coke fizzles on her tongue and, with the sun in her eyes and the river moving in lapping waves, all Cassie's world sits in her mouth. She sighs. This is the happiest she's felt in a long time, certainly today and probably since Mark came home.

Together they make their way through the paper cartons. Hettie Cotter comes out with a damp cloth and wipes down the other picnic table. "Everything all right out here?"

"Thanks Hettie, as good as usual," says Frank.

"You still working for the Greeks, sweetheart?"

"Uh huh."

"That's a big outfit."

"I guess so," answers Cassie.

"They bring clams to Boston?"

"Sometimes," she lies.

"Mm mm," she answers.

After they finish, Frank Leahy wanders down to the wharf and Cassie follows. "The tide's high. Let's take a ride. I want to check out the boat."

The tide is full, so the floating dock sits only inches below the cement wall that separates the river from the parking lot, and the wooden gangplank lies almost flat over the water. Frank keeps his small outboard tied to one end of the float. The space is officially reserved for dinghies, but the harbormaster is a friend, so this transgression is overlooked. All the boats ride high on the full tide, bobbing near the top of the cement wall, and most carry water after the storm. Cassie gets in after her dad, careful not to sink her sneakers under water, and they both bail in silence a few minutes until the cans scrape the bottom and only inches remain. Frank Leahy hooks up the gas tank and then pulls the starter. It sputters a bit, but when it catches Cassie unties the bowline and pushes off the dock. They drift downstream a few feet before the engine catches full hold and then putter slowly along the curve of the river, keeping the wake small for the boats moored along the way. Cassie pulls a life preserver out from under the lines to slip onto the metal seat as a cushion, but it's too soggy to use.

Cassie watches the empty blue sky to the west shading toward sunset. They turn another curve and the river widens. As the river runs to sea, the water lightens and loses its murky brown appearance. The marsh grass is bright green, and as the wind still chops from the storm, the bow dips and rises on small swells. Frank turns up the engine. With the high tide he can head a straight line without worrying about the markers. Cassie holds onto the side of the seat to keep steady. Her hair flies out behind her.

The moving sky, darker in the east, and the insistent wind blowing waves over the green grass reflect the recent storm, but the wind is warm and the falling sun shines low and bright in the west. The rhythm of the waves and the smell of the sea fill Cassie and she closes her eyes and feels her mother calling to her to let her know she's not alone, that she and her father are not alone. She leans back and breathes in the sharp, fresh air, thankful for the water, for the marshes, and for the colors of the sunset that make it possible for her mother to reach her. She opens her eyes and watches her dad scan the horizon. If they weren't chopping through after-storm water, Cassie would go to the stern and give him a hug, to feel his warmth through his flannel shirt.

Frank pulls up as they get to the bay. The wind's still blowing and white caps crest the waves just beyond the mouth. "Too rough on a full stomach," he calls to her from the stern, and he arcs the boat around in a deep and perfect curve back to where their wake still forms a smooth path home. She waves to him and smiles, OK, and he speeds back along the river as the sun turns peach and the sky pink around them.

"Engine check out all right?" she asks her father as they pull in back to the wharf.

"Seems that way," he answers.

She steps back onto the dock and, until she pulls her hair back behind her ears and hurts her tender cheek, she almost forgets that her face is swollen and the topic of conversation. She slowly climbs back up the gangplank toward the pinkened sky.

At home, Mark's car is gone, her bed is empty, her father's shirt slung over a kitchen chair.

### June 23, 1971

Midweek, the wide beach is near empty, just a scattering of mothers and their children.

Dark oval sunglasses, bought an hour earlier at the Woolworth's down the street, hide Cassie's bruise. This morning the eye was ringed in black, the side of her face puffy and red.

She lays down her towel on the soft sand sheltered along the beach grass, nearer the dunes and farther from the water, where the wild wind whips the sand ceaselessly across the beach and sprays mare's tails across the post-storm rollers. Even in her protected inlet, an occasional blast sends a sting of sand against her skin. She turns her head leeward. These early summer rays are almost medicinal and she drinks them in, always, when she is on the beach, thinking of the winter and the store of sun she'll need to take her through the dark months.

This morning, up early in her empty kitchen, her head ached and she knew she'd have to wait until at least tomorrow to try the running shoes.

But on the bike ride to the beach, over the long cool road shaded by grand old trees and then past the sparkling green marsh of the estuary, she felt as if she were pedaling air. And now, her body on the warm sand, eyes closed, with only the wind and the breaking waves to listen to, she feels on the edge of the world and falling toward sleep, all of yesterday and tomorrow gone and only her breathing, here, now.

Cassie isn't sure how long she's been asleep when she turns and stares up to see a stranger, long blonde hair billowing out from her face like Medusa and her head of silky snakes. Next to the stranger is Teri, whose groomed hair slices into the cobalt sky like a face cut out of a photograph with a razor. They both carry aluminum lawn chairs and brightly colored bags, and the stranger, this Nina, carries a large plastic thermos.

"New sunglasses?" asks Teri.

Nina, quickly out of her clothes, stands in her minute white bikini and surveys the beach, which curves miles in both directions. "There's no one here." She bends over to open up her chair and, briefly, it appears as if she's lost the top part of her bathing suit. Where's Stu, thinks Cassie with a smile. He's missing all the fun.

"Nina," snaps Teri, "no one promised you the Riviera."

Nina angles her chair to face the sun, takes out a bottle of baby oil, and rubs generous amounts onto her skin. "I'll go for a walk later," she says. "If there's anyone here, I'll find him." When her body's oiled, she takes out a radio, tunes it close to her ear, and then places it by her chair. The wind's blowing the music away from Cassie, but snatches of what sounds like the Fifth Dimension drift in her direction.

Teri peels down to a demure, navy blue bikini dotted with white daisies. She leaves her chair and lays her towel down next to Cassie. "What happened to your face?" she whispers.

"Huh?"

"Come on, Cass, I bet you've got a contusion four inches in diameter under those sunglasses."

Cassie glances at Nina. Her head tilts back, face toward the sun, chair angled away from their towels. She wonders if Teri would believe the freezer story and then wonders why she just can't tell Teri the truth.

"It was an accident."

"Well," she laughs. "I certainly didn't think you were in a fistfight." She reaches into her bag for a tube of suntan lotion, the oily bronze kind with a distinctive scent. *For the St. Tropez Tan!* it says on the label.

"It was a freezer at work."

"I love that smell!" gushes Nina. "Hand it over when you're done."

"A freezer?" asks Teri.

"There's something wrong with the handle. It doesn't always catch right when you open it and I opened it wrong. Don't worry, though. George is ordering a new one. This was the last straw for him."

"It's pretty swollen. Did you ice it?" Teri sits up to rub the lotion on her legs and Cassie is suddenly glad for her lie.

"I iced it."

"You should have iced it longer." She hands the tube to Nina, who squeezes liberal globs onto her chest.

"I love this song," shouts Nina. She turns up the volume of her radio, sings and snaps her fingers: "Busted down in Baton Rouge, waitin' for a train, feeling near as faded as my jeans.'"

Cassie doesn't know which is worse, that she and Nina both love the same song, or listening to Nina sing over Janis. She rolls over and joins in: "'Bobby hailed a diesel down, just before it rained, we rode it all the way to New Orleans.'"

"Sing it, Cassie!" Nina calls out.

"'Freedom's just another word for nothing left to lose,'" Nina and Cassie sing the song through together and by the end Teri, too, rolls onto her back and sings to the sky with them: "'I'd trade all my tomorrows for a single yesterday, when I was holding Bobby's body next to mine . . . me and my Bobby McGee.'"

The guitars and drum and Janis end with a thump, and Nina quickly turns the radio down. "Can't stand to pollute Janis."

Cassie smiles.

"I forgot you two had that in common," says Teri.

"What?" says Nina. She kicks Teri's leg with her foot. It

slides a bit along her calf in the suntan oil.

"The worshipping dead singers thing."

"Not any dead singer."

"Just Janis." Nina holds up her fingers in a "V" and waves her hand from side to side and smiles at Cassie. Cassie smiles back, without the "V."

"She's still just a singer."

"Yes sir, Dr. Pinter," says Nina.

"Dr. Pinter," says Cassie. "That sounds right."

"You better believe it," says Nina.

Warm in the sun, Cassie takes off her shorts and her shirt. She rolls off her towel and onto the sand so that her skin can drink up the warmth of the millions of grains beneath her.

"That's the same suit you wore last year," says Teri. "You need a new one every year, I've told you that a million times, Cassie."

"With those muscles, she can wear anything," says Nina. "Where did you get all those muscles?"

At first impulse Cassie wants to ignore the question, but the spirit of friendship demands otherwise. "I don't know," she answers. "Working, most likely."

Nina reaches into her bag and pulls out cups. "Anyone want some?"

"No," says Teri.

"I will." Cassie reaches over as Nina hands her a paper cup filled with cold red liquid. One sip tells her that it's Kool-Aid spiked with vodka.

They lie still for a while, and then Nina stretches out of her chair, fingertips raised toward the sky. "Time to explore."

Once she's out of earshot, Teri says, "You don't want to drink that."

"It's just got some vodka in it."

"That's what you can taste, but seriously, Cass, you don't know what else she put in there."

Cassie sniffs at the cup. "I could ask her."

"She won't tell. She claims it's about trust."

"She's not so bad after all. She's kind of fun."

"I'm just not sure why she's still here. She says she wants to work with my father every day. They think she's great, everything I'm not, outgoing, charming, a go-getter."

"Forget your parents. She's your friend."

"I did get lab work, though, in Cambridge. The commute's gonna be a nightmare."

A seagull cries above them, a splash of white and sound in vast blue.

"I got new running sneakers. They're the latest technology and this guy I met in the store told me that some schools have spots for girls who will run for them. So I'm running again."

"You don't need to run to go to college. You just have to decide to go and find a place where you can transfer credits. Or just forget the credits and find a place."

"I like to run."

"You were really good at it," Teri concedes.

"At Cosmo . . ."

"Cass, Cosmo's is just a job. You need to get out of that place."

Just a job, being a doctor is just a job, Cassie could respond. But she knows Teri means well. Balls of sweat condense and roll behind Cassie's knees and under her arms. She sits up, drains the paper cup and heads for the water. "I'm boiling. I need to go for a swim."

She heads across the soft sand above the high tide line toward the water. Sand stings her ankles and legs in the steady breeze. Below the high tide line errant loose sand skitters along the hard-packed surface, and the wind sends shimmers over the shallow waters that pool in the bowls after the waves break. No sandpipers dart in and out of the shallows on their spindly legs today, and only the gulls ride the high drafts above her.

The water's always cold. Except for late August and early September, any dip is bracing at best. Now, June, the water is frigid and as she passes over the wet sand she is less inclined to want to step in. An icy wave catches her toes and she jumps back. The only way to do this is to dive straight in, so she trots back ten feet, takes off her sunglasses, holds them in her hand and runs hard, letting the chilled water splash up to her knees before she dives in head first. Breath held, sounds muffled, motion fluid, any immersion under water is a visit to a place of solitude and then, with a gasp of air, she's up again, shivering. She jogs through the surf back to dry sand.

"Jesus, what happened to you?"

Cassie blinks in the sun. It's Nina.

"Wait right here, don't move," she says, running back to the towels.

Cassie twists the water out of her hair, gently rubs the salt out her eyes with the pads of her fingers and faces the sun.

"Look over here."

Nina is back, and Cassie turns, face over her right shoulder, hands up by her neck, caught by surprise. Nina cradles a camera and with alarming rapidity clicks off a series of shots as she turns the camera from side to side and walks around Cassie. No, Cassie thinks, stop, but she is too taken aback to find her words. Cassie turns to follow the camera, shaking her head, and then she thinks to put her sunglasses back on. Nina takes a few more shots and lowers the camera.

She peers through the view once more and recaps the lens. "There's so much ambient light here, I had to set the speed faster but I can't be sure of the shadows, you know? You never know the whole story 'til you see the negative."

Cassie's heart beats in gallops. The wind gusts and she shivers, rubs her hands over her upper arms. Nina holds up her camera and takes a few more shots. "Being all wet like that, it's like you're naked or something. These'll be great."

"What?" Cassie finally manages.

"Oh," says Nina, "you wouldn't know. For my portfolio." She turns a knob on the camera. "I'll let you know if I mount them in a show or something, you know, pain into art and all that."

Anger carries her. "That's bullshit."

Nina holds the camera down and looks straight at Cassie. "You know what's bullshit? Letting someone smack you around, that's bullshit."

"No one smacked me around."

Nina glances up toward the dunes. "She may believe that freezer crap. You could at least come up with something better. Unless it's your first time and you can't think of anything else." She turns back to Cassie and tilts her head toward her shoulder. "Try again. What happened?"

Cassie's mood lurches between loathing and a desolating feeling of loneliness. She looks out through the sunshine over the waves to the horizon—sky over water, blue over blue, motion over motion, light over dark, and air over water. Where would she begin? From before, just to kiss him and ride around in his old car together? From when his number was called and he never, not for a second, wanted to go, but he went? From the way he runs at her and away from her since he came home? From the way he handled her in the alley by the river?

"He didn't mean to hurt me. He was asleep and his arm just swung out from a nightmare."

"Who?"

Cassie focuses. If only she could get the story out in a sentence, maybe then she could look at it for a while and know it for what it was.

"Mark. I used to be with him, but then he went to Vietnam and now ..." She snorts. "He's kind of a mess. But he's only been back a few weeks or so."

"What did he say when it happened?"

"He doesn't know."

Nina is surprised. "He's gotta know."

"Like I said, he's pretty much upset all the time anyway."

"Too bad for him."

Cassie starts walking back toward her towel.

Nina walks along with her. "Look. He was probably into some evil shit over there, but that's not your problem."

Teri sits up.

Cassie turns toward Nina. "They fight for us over there."

Nina holds up her palm. "No one's fighting for me."

"He didn't want to go."

"He could have gone to Canada."

He could have gone to Mars, thinks Cassie, but she's tired again and lies down on her towel.

"Look," says Teri, "my mother made us sandwiches. I think she put mayonnaise on them so we should eat them soon." Teri unpacks three square packages wrapped tightly in tin foil, opens them up, and puts one on Cassie's towel, one on Nina's lap, and keeps one for herself. Cassie turns her head, sniffs at the efficient sandwich cut evenly into four, and rapidly chews one triangle after another.

Nina pours Kool-Aid into a cup, nibbles at her sandwich, and then hands it back. "I think there's sand in mine."

"Maybe you would have gone to Canada," says Teri. "Maybe I would have gone to Canada. But some people can't pack up and leave everything they've ever known."

The sandwich Cassie just ate propels itself back up her throat and she sits up quickly. Mark would never have gone to Canada and left her. And she never made it easier for him, offered to go with him. They had never even talked about it.

"Are you OK? Are you dizzy? Maybe you got a concussion."

Cassie shakes her head, "The sandwich."

"Forgawdsakes, I told my mother to put mustard on them." Teri turns and stretches out her hand toward Nina who's picked up her camera again. "I'll rip the film out, I swear!"

Nina laughs.

"I'm going for a walk," says Cassie.

Teri gets up. "I'll come too. Diane Arbus can stay here."

Nina, her head back and her eyes closed, doesn't respond.

They walk southward along the shore that goes miles along the ocean before it reaches around like the bend of an arm into another river and spreads its fingers through the marshes. The wind blows alongside and sends the cold tide over their feet at uneven intervals. The day is sunny and beautiful and quiet. After a mile or so, they head up into the soft sand and lie down on their stomachs.

Cassie thinks, I could tell Teri anything here, but she can't begin to find the thoughts, can't bring herself to relate the details, any one of which would make Teri tell her to run, run hard in the other direction, away from Mark, away from here.

She puts her cheek in the warm sand. "This is the real reason I won't leave," says Cassie. "This beach, this sun, this quiet. It's all I really know."

"This place just gives you the illusion that nothing changes. But things are always changing." Teri turns on her back and tilts her face to the sun. "Plus, Ipswich'll still be here when you come back."

"But will it be the same for me? If I leave it?"

She sighs. "Cassandra Anne Leahy, homebody."

"Teri Swanson Pinter, world traveler."

It is deep into the afternoon by the time the girls make their way down the boardwalk toward the parking lot. Cassie picks up her bike from the rack and walks Teri and Nina to the car, reluctant to ride too quickly over the rocky gravel lest she pop a tire. She is making her way out of the lot when she hears a horn beep four times in a row. She stops, one foot on the ground and turns back. Nina, still wearing only her slight bikini, stands by the car waving and shouting her name.

"We're stuck," she wails.

Cassie pedals back, puts down the kickstand, and walks over to the driver's side. "What is it?"

"I don't know, Cass. It won't start."

"Turn the key."

Teri turns the key in the ignition. It clicks, but the engine's quiet.

"Battery's gone," says Cassie. "Or it could be the alternator. Did you leave the lights on? Or anything?"

"I don't think so."

Nina's bathing suit has ridden way up, and she hops a little to release herself.

"We could call Stu," says Cassie. "You know, the guy who was in our class and came over to talk to us at the pub?"

"Would he come?"

"He works at White's. It's his job."

"Is he cute?" asks Nina.

Cassie pedals over to the pay phone. Before she dials, she sends Stu a telepathic message to answer the ringing phone. "Stu," she says when she hears his voice. "Remember that blonde you saw in the pub? The one who was with me?"

He is instantly on board. "Yeah?"

"She's here at the beach, in a bikini way too small for her, and she's been drinking vodka and Kool-Aid all day in the hot sun."

"Cassie, why are you torturing me?"

"Because," she waits a beat, "her car's broken down and she needs a tow!"

"Ohmygod," he answers and hangs up.

Cassie pedals back to the car.

"Is he coming?" asks Teri. She has set up her beach chair to face the afternoon sun.

"Yup."

"Will he be here soon?"

Cassie looks over at Nina, who's sprawled on the front seat, head back and eyes closed. "I expect so."

Within minutes, White's tow truck zooms across the nearly empty lot. When Stu steps out of the driver's seat, Cassie is pleased to see that he's taken off his work overalls and wears a T-shirt tucked into jeans and some dark sunglasses. His bulk looks like strength in these clothes, and when Nina gets out of the front seat, tilts her hip, and puts her hand over her eyebrows to get a closer look at him, what Cassie recognizes as tongue-tied could easily be mistaken for confident silence.

"The ignition won't turn," says Cassie. "You could check the battery or the alternator."

He tears his eyes away from Nina and moves to reach his hand in under the dashboard to lift the hood. "Yup," he says after a minute. He sounds gleeful. "You're stuck."

Nina walks over to the front of the car. "Show me," she says.

Stu takes a step back, wipes his forehead with a patterned bandana from his back pocket. "There," he points. "That's where the belt is, see?"

"No, I don't see."

He steps closer to her. They both lean under the hood. "See, there's the belt, and there, see it's frayed. It's what charges the car to start and so that's why the key don, uh, doesn't work."

"So, you can replace the belt?" asks Teri.

Stu steps back from the hood. He runs his bandana over his forehead again. "Sure, but we've gotta tow the car in first. Then we'll take a better look and see what we've got in stock."

"Maybe I should call my mother."

"Why? I think this guy's got everything under control. Don't you, uh . . ." Nina peers at Stu's chest. "Hey! Why don't you have your name on your shirt?"

"His name is Stu," says Cassie.

Nina holds her hand out, wrist bent, fingers arched downward. "I'm Nina."

Stu looks at his work boots, and they all follow his stare at the wide rubber soles and shiny brass rivets until he touches the tips of Nina's fingers gingerly between his thumb and forefingers.

"You remember Teri," says Cassie.

Teri waves.

"Yeah, sure, how's it going Dr. Teri?"

Stu retreats to the truck to angle it in for the tow with Nina on his heels, stepping lightly over the gravel in her bare feet. When it's time to lift the car, he lets her push the hydraulics.

Despite Cassie's protests, Stu lifts her bicycle onto the back and the four of them squeeze into the front, but not until Nina takes some photos of Stu climbing into the cab, eyeglasses glinting into the side-view mirror. "Very Yang," she says, "you know. Lots of metal and glass." On the ride to White's, Nina and Stu carry on a steady conversation. Cassie can't make out what they're saying over the sound of the oversized engine and the rattle of the tow chains through the open windows.

"What are they talking about?" she whispers to Teri.

"Do you think I'm listening?" Teri snaps back.

"Come on, tell me," presses Cassie, suspicious because she can't remember the last time Stu strung so many sentences together.

Back at the garage, triangled as it is by busy streets, every other passing car shouts out something to Nina until even she is tired of the attention and decides to put her clothes back on. They sit on the curb in the shade of the tow truck while Stu checks the parts inventory.

"I should call my mother," says Teri.

Stu emerges from the bays holding a cardboard box. "We've got what we need. Mr. White's not here right now, so I can fix it . . ." He pauses and Cassie puts her hand up to her face to push her sunglasses up only to remember she'd taken off her sunglasses while they sat in the shade. "What happened to you?"

"She ran into the freezer at work," say Teri and Nina in unison.

Cassie looks down at the pitted gravel beneath her feet and smiles, unaccountably pleased with the lie.

"It looks like someone belted you." Stu stares down at her. Even if he believes the story, he is not happy about it.

"Black eyes tend to show similar characteristics no matter what the specifics of the impact."

"OK, Dr. Teri," he says.

"The alternator," prompts Cassie.

"Yeah, I can fix that. You want to wait?"

"How long?" Teri asks.

Stu hesitates. "Like I said, Mr. White's out on a job, so I can move it to the front and have it in and out before he comes back."

Teri persists. "An hour?"

"We can wait at my house," says Cassie. "Stu can just call us when it's done."

"Or you could bring it by," says Nina.

Stu smiles. "Or I could bring it by."

"What about payment?" continues Teri.

"He can bill your mother, right, Stu?"

He nods at Teri.

Teri and Nina head for the sidewalk, toward Cassie's house.

"Write down this address," Cassie orders Stu.

"I don't care about . . ."

"Save your favors. Her parents can afford it."

"What's with the eye, Cass?"

"I told you already."

He grabs her arm as she turns to follow her friends. "Cass," he whispers, "do you know what the hell you're doing?"

She pulls her arm away, suddenly hot and sweaty and annoyed. "Of course I don't," she hisses, "but what am I supposed to do about it?"

"I should call my mother,"Teri is saying when Cassie catches up. "This kind of thing always flips her out."

"But your dad's going to like that you took care of it, Teri. You know," Nina deepens her voice, "find the problem and then solve it."

Cassie laughs.

"See," says Nina, "Cassie knows I'm right."

They reach the house and head on down the drive.

"She never locks her house," says Teri. "Anyone who comes here once is welcome forever after."

"There's nothing to steal," says Cassie.

"There's always something to steal," says Nina.

The three of them walk through the back door.

Nina passes a cool eye over the cluttered countertops, the piles on the floor and on the chairs, and Cassie imagines a camera in her hands. "I guess your mother's not Betty Crocker."

Teri opens her mouth, but Cassie interrupts. "I guess not." She goes to the freezer and pulls out three freeze pops.

"That's cool," says Nina, her mouth bright red from the Kool-Aid. "Liberated women aren't tied to their houses."

Cassie hands her a blue pop. Maybe it'll mix with the red and make her mouth purple, she thinks. At the least it may shut her up. She gives Teri her favorite, the orange, vitamin C and all that, and keeps the red for herself.

Teri lets the pop sit on the table. "Cassie's mother died when she was five."

Nina looks genuinely alarmed. She leans forward. "I'm sorry. I'm too flip for my own good."

"Yes you are," says Teri, "too flip for your own good."

Cassie gets up and turns on the radio. It's only the news and so she turns it off again. She looks over to the counter and peers into the wooden boxes Mark made. The white eggs he left a few days earlier have become tiny green worms, and they've eaten a few bitty holes out of the leaves.

"I know what I'll do." Nina stands up. "I'll make dinner."

Cassie looks at Nina and wants to laugh. Her face and arms are sunburned red, her mouth is a funny color, maybe purple, and her hair is wild around her head. She likes her better this way. "My dad usually makes dinner."

"He deserves a night off."

Cassie turns to Teri.

"She can cook. I'd let her."

"And in return you can take me to your friend's house so I can see the car he's working on."

Stu?" asks Cassie.

"Yeah, I think I can help him out."

"With the car?"

"Not with the insides, but with the outside."

"Stu?" echoes Teri.

"Sure. I know some serious paint stores in town." Nina smiles. "He's a real diamond in the rough."

Cassie turns her back. What's that supposed to mean, she fumes.

"What about it?" asks Nina.

"Dinner is yours," answers Cassie. "The fridge and the cabinets too."

When her dad comes home and finds extra girls in his kitchen, his face lights up with pleasure. Cassie is annoyed with the self-mocking way he excuses his own entrance and how easily he surrenders his domain. Then, clean and changed, he comes back into the kitchen, grabs himself a beer, and sits down like a guest in his own house. Maybe they both need some more variation in their days, thinks Cassie, something other than the routine that keeps them comfortable and afloat.

As Teri sets the plates on the table to eat, Cassie hears a door slam.

"Maybe that's Stu with the car!" calls out Nina.

But when Cassie looks out the door, there is no one there. She walks to the end of the drive, only to see Mark's car pull out. She wants to run after the car and shout, I'll go with you! I'll go to Canada!

Back in the kitchen, her dad asks, "Who was there?"

"No one," she answers. "Just someone turning around."

"Well," says Nina as she carries a large plate of pork chops and onions to the table, "whoever wants to join us, there's certainly extra here."


Later that evening, Cassie finds her father sitting on the step, with the back door light off. "Dad," she calls through the screen door.

"Take at look at this."

She turns on the light.

"No, keep the light off."

She opens the door slowly to accommodate her father on the step. Outside, the air is cooler, and although the breeze is almost gone, the dark is far from still. He pats the spot next to him. She sits down. "Look up," he says.

"Why?"

"Shh."

They sit for a few minutes in silence, both staring up at the clear night sky. The house blocks the streetlights in front, leaving the backyard dark enough to see the cluster of stars hovering over the trees. Cassie blinks. A sliver of light cuts through the dark.

"Did you see that one?"

"I did."

"Wait, they've been coming every few minutes or so."

Mark would like this. So many times they sat on the beach at night, in all temperatures, waiting for the stars to fall.

"There's another one," says Cassie.

They fall in a shower and then more time passes between the meteors. Frank Leahy leans back against the screen door and drinks the last of his beer. "Well," he says.

The leaves swish overhead and a car goes by in front of the house. "Those college girls are as much fun as they're made out to be, aren't they?"

I'm a college girl, too, she wants to remind him, but that's not what he means.

"I used to think that maybe Mark was the reason you didn't go off to school."

"Just because I'm smart doesn't mean I have to be a doctor."

He laughs. "One doctor's enough for one kitchen. Your mother…"

Cassie feels the blood in her veins stop for a pulse before it continues on its way. He hardly ever mentions her mother.

"Your mother, she'd have gone to college. If she could."

Cassie nods, her eyes on the gray of the fence on the other side of the tracks.

"Just don't stick around on my account."

"What, you think you're that much fun?" she says when she's able.

He stands and they go into the house, but not before Frank Leahy turns around and takes one last look at the sky, in case he should miss something while his back is turned.

## June 25, 1971

"Take a right here, onto Poorfarm," says Cassie from the back seat.

"Poorfarm!" Nina adjusts the sun visor, then quickly flips down the mirror to smooth her hair. "What kind of road is that?"

Out the window, Cassie watches the scrubby pines that cluster in patches along the twisting road. Her father told her years ago, in response to a similar question, that Poorfarm Road earned its name during the depression when a farm for people with nowhere else to go was placed at the end of it, just before the town dump.

"I mean, really," continues Nina, "talk about bad karma."

"There's a road on the way to the beach called Heartbreak," says Teri.

"Whose heart?"

Teri shrugs. "I don't know."

Cassie remembers another local story of an Indian maiden who had lost her lover to either a ship or a war, and then wandered the paths atop the hill behind the road that bears that name, scanning the ocean for her lover's return.

"Cassie's dad knows all that kind of stuff. Do you know the story?" she asks.

Cassie, more concerned about Nina's plans for Stu, isn't in the mood to play tour guide. She points to Stu's house. "Pull over here."

Although the town dump is a good half-mile past Stu's

house and usually can't be smelled from that distance, the condition of his front yard does little to reduce the impression of proximity to disorder and waste. The lawn is rarely cut, and even when newly mown the short stems only serve to highlight the vast brown areas of dead grass. The walk, once evenly poured cement squares, is cracked and hosts the only flowers in the area: dandelions, daisies, and wild violets, all undersized and tough in their bright, fighting colors.

Stu's the youngest of a brood long flown away. The house is often empty and the kitchen ill provisioned but even during its best and busiest years, you would never expect lemonade on a hot day, or after-school cookies. With his father gone to Florida almost three years now, his mother is on a schedule that alternates exclusively between her job as cashier at the A&P and the living room couch. Cassie has often wondered how Stu ever managed to get himself through high school.

As they pull up, Stu races out from the open garage before Teri has turned off the engine. Cassie fears he'll circle the car like a big, overeager puppy until they get out, but Stu manages to stand still and say nothing until all the car doors slam.

"You all came!" he shouts out, as if he can't believe his own luck.

They squint in the shadeless sun. A seagull cries out from overhead, its call quickly followed by a cascade of shots that ring out one-two-three-four into the quiet of the front yard. All heads turn toward the house.

"That's my mother. She likes to watch Gunsmoke in the afternoons."

"So," prompts Nina.

Stu turns and heads down the hardened dirt drive that curves around the back. Nina totters behind on the high, thick heels of her flowered plastic sandals.

The grass in the backyard also makes no pretense towards cultivation. It grows in tall, random clumps, save the area around the car and the path to a weather-beaten shed where the weeds are worn down to the dirt. No spare parts or metal pieces litter Stu's workspace, and a neat row of cinder blocks stands sentry to one side. Cassie can't see any signs of his last car, a heavy wagon of mostly Ford parts he sold to a customer of Mr. White's. Stu painted that one a glistening green, she remembers, without any help from Nina, the self-styled artist for all occasions. Cassie plunks herself down on one of the cinder blocks.

This latest car is long and lean. Although patched in a thousand places with a rusty-colored spray paint, it looks as if it would be fast and sleek on the road. Stu runs his hand over the roof. "It's an Eldorado chassis, and I've got some chrome sidepieces I can put on when the time comes. I got this V8 off an old Chevy, 315 horse at 56 rpms. Sure, it has its problems, but it's easy to get parts for. The right wheels were a bitch to find, but Mark hooked me up with some buddy of his in New Hampshire he knew from over there, and he got me four matches, at a cellar price, because I was a friend of his, of Mark's, I mean. This same guy can get Caddy covers too."

"An Eldorado?" says Nina. A wide blue headband keeps the hair off her face and gives her a mature, serious look that Cassie has to remind herself to ignore.

"I know," says Stu, who doesn't respond to Nina's condescension. "Do you know how hard it is to find body parts like that? I really lucked out."

Nina sneers. "That's so square! What's the point of making an Eldorado when you could just go out and buy one!"

Cassie half gets up off her cinder block to defend him, but Stu shrugs his shoulders. "I couldn't buy one," he concedes. "And besides," he thumps the hood, "I like my cars solid so they can take me places in comfort and style."

"You sound like my dad," laughs Teri.

"Really?" says Stu. "Maybe he'd be interested in this one, if

I decide I want to let it go." He looks toward Teri, but she avoids his hopeful gaze to sit on the cinder block next to Cassie.

Nina turns her eyes from the car to the tattered roof of Stu's ranch-style house. Cassie is glad she isn't toting her camera, to snap a thousand photos of Stu's wrecked home so she could then hang them in some show where everyone could come and comment and gawk. Not everything is a choice, she wants to remind her.

Nina walks slowly around the car, her plastic heels tippy on the beaten hard ground. "What color?" she asks.

"I haven't decided. What do you think?"

"How about some naked women along the sides?"

"You should have seen her drawings of the cadavers," whispers Teri. She shifts carefully on her cinder block, stretching her thin legs in front for balance. "She got in big trouble for them, almost got kicked out of the class."

"Why?"

"She wasn't supposed to draw them. They thought she wasn't taking the dead seriously."

Stu runs his hand over his forehead. "Jesus, Nina," he says, "I don't think so."

"How about a dragon?" Nina suggests.

"A dragon?"

"With an open orange mouth and wings and scales in different shades of blue and green, it could be fantastic!" She circles the car, lays her palms down on the hood. "See, we could put the head and mouth here, and wrap the wings along the sides."

"You can do that?"

"I don't have my brushes with me, so I'd need to buy some, along with the right paint. What do you use?" She kneels in the grass and moves her fingers along the scarred doors as Stu bends over her.

Teri hisses in undertones, "I bet she doesn't even have an

uncle in Italy."

The back door swings open, letting out the sound of a television laugh track and a woman with wispy gray hair, in lime green pants and an oversized T-shirt. She blinks in the slanted afternoon light. "Cassie, is that you?"

"Hi, Mrs. Camineau."

"How's that handsome father of yours?"

"He's the same, he's fine."

"I seen your boyfriend a lot lately," she says with a hint of singsong in her voice.

"Yeah?" Cassie hasn't seen Mark since he hit her, and she pushes away the image of the two of them, Mark and Mrs. Camineau, beers in hand, slouched on the couch, watching Gunsmoke together, and then maybe The Virginian or Perry Mason after that.

"Yeah."

Stu and Nina disappear along the far side of the car.

"It's a good thing to fight for your country. Not all the boys will do that nowadays."

Fighting for his country, is that what he was doing? Mrs. Camineau probably heard that line on some TV show. Cassie doesn't remember Mark writing anything about why he was in Vietnam. It was obvious to the both of them. He was drafted.

"Am I right?" Mrs. Camineau insists.

"Sure, Mrs. Camineau," answers Cassie quickly, but Mrs. Camineau's already retreating back into the house. The screen door slams behind her. So this is where Mark has been, when he isn't not-sleeping in his own basement. She looks out over the tired grass, toward the shallow woods of bushes and pine. It would be quiet here almost all the time, and he could watch the birds on their way to the dump. She wonders if Stu has been cleaning up the beer bottles.

"It's all set then," says Stu to Nina. He calls out to Cassie, "It's all set!"

Cassie nods and waves her hand.

"What are they talking about?" Teri asks her. Cassie shrugs. She stands to follow Nina and Stu along back to the car.

"I can go into Boston tomorrow to get the paints and brushes I need. You have to spray that base on, like we talked about, as soon as you can, right?"

"Not a problem," he says. He hooks his thumbs into his belt loops and grins at Cassie and Teri.

"Nice to see you again Stu," Teri calls out as she gets back into the driver's seat. "And my mother's car runs great ever since you fixed it."

Stu grins again. Once Nina is on her way to the passenger seat, he calls to Cassie in a low voice, "Cassie!"

Cassie turns around. His faded yellow T-shirt hangs low over his baggy jeans, and she wants to tell him to go buy a belt and tuck his shirt in. "What now?"

His eyes blink at her irritation, but he chooses to ignore it like you might ignore the temperature on a hot day; there is nothing to be done about it. "Thanks, Cassie."

"For what?"

"For giving me a chance with her." She wants to shake him, or tell him to wake up, that the chances are a million to one that Stu will end up with a fire-breathing dragon on the hood of his new car, and three billion to one that Nina will remember his name at the end of the month, but the wind shifts and Cassie sniffs the burnt-coffee odor of the dump. Stu's eyes are wide in anticipation and his mouth half open in happiness, and she finds she doesn't want to hurt that face. She pats him on the arm. "I told you you're a good catch."

Back in the car, Nina pulls down the passenger visor again and adjusts her hair beneath her headband in the small mirror attached. "I have to get to Boston. I'll never get just the right paints in these boondocks. And then, of course, I'll need to access some of my bank accounts." She turns to smile at Teri. "It looks like I'll be going to work with your dad again tomorrow."

"So, Nina," Cassie snaps, her voice unable to control the malicious roil of emotions spilling out of her mouth. "When are you going to Italy?"

Nina snaps the visor back into place. "I don't know," she laughs. "There's so much for me to do here!"

## June 27, 1971

There is no one home. Maybe the Sox are on the west coast, or maybe her father has taken his boat down river and is listening to the game on the radio, a red sea worm on a hook hung over the side, waiting for the fish to bite. Cassie throws on her red running shorts and new running shoes and gets onto her bike in a matter of minutes. She rides the four miles to Bradley Palmer Forest in a blur, leaves her bike behind a tree, heads out on the first needle-strewn path she sees, and begins to run, slack, unstrung.

She knows why that boy she met in the shoe store chooses to run here. The woods are alive and humming with an audience of insects, twittering squirrels, and birds, and the ground is soft, easy on her feet. Unlike the relentless round of the track with its repetitive curves and counting of laps, here there is no end or beginning in sight, only the shifting shade and sun and sudden tree roots to occupy her mind. Cassie feels as if she will run forever; this is one of those effortless days when running is as easy as breathing, like the day three years ago when buttercups lined the track and she broke the school record in the eight-eighty and met Mark.

She runs a long time, letting her legs go loose and her breathing take its own rhythm. As the sun shifts west, the forest shades darker, and Cassie loops around in a direction that feels like heading back. When she figures she's got about fifteen minutes left to go, she recognizes the beginning of the trail and spots the tree that hides her bike.

Her legs feel heavy and tired. She leans against a broad trunk and sits down into the soft pine-needle bed that rings the tree. The shadows crawl deeper into the trees and the birds, squirrels, and insects begin to quiet. She closes her eyes.

Cassie remembers Mr. Parker, her high school track coach. Rumored to be a wide receiver back in his college days who had set school records in the two-twenty, she knew him as fleshy, thin haired, and slow moving. As a track coach he had been kind but he'd driven them hard. He had fought to let the girl's team use the football weight room in the off-season, but even so a lot of the girls had looked at the sessions as a waste of time, not worth the effort of another shower. "So, hot feet," he had said to her near the end of her senior season, "did you check out any of those schools I recommended?" She had shrugged her shoulders, and disappointment had colored his skin like ink to water.

Cassie opens her eyes to speak to a vast purple-orange sky and silent woods. "Look, Mr. Parker," she says, "I wasn't ready before."

## June 29, 1971

Under a cloudless summer-blue sky, Cassie pedals her bike deftly among the mahogany-red maples scattered along the edge of the Cosmo lot. Small green seedlings spiral and zoom like helicopters around her in the dappled shade, then fall to rest in the gravel.

Cassie lifts up off her seat and rides slowly over the small rocks. Leaning her bike in her usual spot against the front wall, she resists the urge to park it in the back to see which cars are in the lot. If George, or even Cosmo, were there, they would know she is late, the morning spent running.

The new brass front door lock, special ordered from a locksmith after the robbery, gleams in the sun. That she was the first one into Cosmo on the morning of the robbery remains a secret between her and David. Cassie fingers her worn house key that she still carries in the dip of her pocket. Maybe she should stop carrying her old key, to prevent herself from unlocking things she shouldn't.

Today the front door opens easily. The cavernous quiet and dull cold are familiar, but when the bright force of overhead bulbs hits she knows that only David is here. No one but David would flip on all these lights for no good reason.

Cosmo is overexposed; the metal roof appears jagged and harsh, the pine shelving crude, the secondhand freezers dented and faded, and the cement floor chipped and badly in need of a new coat of paint. She'd like to switch the bulbs off, click, click, click, click, and dark. Chilly, she pulls on her hooded navy blue sweatshirt. Maybe Teri is right, maybe she should be thinking about another job.

She finds David, whom she hasn't seen since their encounter in the truck, bent over some paperwork in the office. Arms stretched wide to the side like the limbs of a scale, he's dribbling imaginary basketballs. Still looking at the desk, he talks to her, his voice confidential, intimate even. "I had this guy call this morning for mussels. They see Cosmo Shellfish and they think we have everything." He peeks up. His grandfather's dark eyes narrow in an evaluative squint, he stops his dribbling, and his mouth twists. "What happened to you?"

The classical Greeks idolized perfection in form. Mr. Brooks' words, from a lesson on Aphrodite maybe, come to her, as if the ancient Greeks' predilection for beauty could serve to cover her own surprise at being hurt, almost shamed by David's reaction to what was only a black eye, after all. She can't help but think that Mark wouldn't react this way, that Mark would be more forgiving. At the same time she remembers that Mark is responsible for the injury in the first place.

"How does a girl get a bruise like that, on her face, for chrisakes?"

"Technically, shellfish does include mussels, so you can see why people call."

"What?"

"There are lots of places in Canada, like Prince Edward Island, that harvest tons of mussels."

He shakes his head, dismissive. "Jesus, Cassie. I don't get you."

This last remark cuts as deep as his obvious disgust at her injured face, perhaps because it is true. "Furthermore, many restaurants call here asking for them but your great-uncle feels that mussels are best left to peasants." She spits this last word out, like an Armenian grandmother cursing the Turks, bitter words into a clean kitchen sink.

David glances from side to side, eyes wide and empty,

searching for a way out of the small office that doesn't involve passing Cassie at the door.

Cassie can't march by him and grab the checkbook for the weighing because George still hasn't given her the new safe combination. She would like to think it was because he forgot, but perhaps he was waiting for her to quit and get married to her returning soldier boyfriend.

She and David would never run Cosmo Shellfish as some kind of team. He had only reached for her in the truck, in the rain, like a drowning person climbs over bodies to reach air. Maybe her not being part of the family, not being Greek, being a girl, have brought her to a dead end.

She turns and heads to the utility room to make a pot of coffee.

On her way, she snaps off a few of the lights. If David notices, he says nothing.

While the coffee perks, she hoses down the bays. Then she hoses the mud-splattered buckets.

Cassie thinks about the restaurants that have telephoned asking for different sorts of shellfish, as well as a chef or two she knows by name, about her list of mussel and shellfish distributors in Canada. I could double this business in a year, David, she thinks, but if you're in charge, then be in charge.

She turns off the hose. In the resulting quiet, rivulets of water snake their way toward the drains. The back door opens, and this sends a wide, bright shaft of light across the floor like an arrow. Cassie looks up.

Freddo gently hauls a bursting red mesh bag over his shoulder, resting it down with a mild grunt. He pulls at his jeans, which have slipped down his straight hips. His red bandana, wrapped over his head, gives him a jaunty appearance, like a pirate, despite his muddy boots and sodden pant legs. "Goddamn greenheads are coming," he says.

"Freddo, I've never seen one before the Fourth of July."

"I take no chances with those fuckers. They'd eat the fuckin' nose off your face if you let 'em."

She laughs. He glances several times at her eye. "So," he hesitates, "he ready to go here?"

"I'm not in charge anymore."

He turns, quick and angry. "Did the Greeks do that to you?"

Cassie has no doubt that if she told him David had hit her, Freddo would be in the office before the words left her lips. She wonders what he would do if she told him he had kissed her, nothing more, in the cab of the refrigerator truck.

"No, this was an accident. And David, well," she can't resist a jab at him, "he's playing boss today, and I don't have the checkbook."

"Well, Cassie, what did you expect? Sooner or later he was gonna figure out that his dad owns the place."

The back door opens with a bang against the wall, and Andy Faragut stands for a second silhouetted in the threshold before he heaves two bushels onto the ground. Cassie winces at the sound of cracking shells and takes a quick note, if he's got two overfull bags, one must be yesterday's tide.

"Fuck," he says. He looks up at Cassie. "Huh," he laughs grimly, "I'd say your boyfriend's back."

Her first instinct is to ball up her fist and ram it into his face but, just as quickly, she pulls back, upset at the violence of her anger. I'm no better than the rest of them, she thinks. She turns her back on him and walks toward the office.

"Hey, let's get the show on the road!" Andy yells after her.

She ignores him.

David remains seated at the desk, staring at some point on the ceiling. Although Dodie and Paul are due any moment to load up the trucks, the loading and delivery sheets are not completed, and no one has transported any bushels from the freezers to the docks. I'm not in charge, Cassie reminds herself, and I am not his girlfriend.

"David!"

His head rocks forward. "Oh. Cassie."

Andy Faragut moves in behind Cassie. "I don't have all day."

"Why not?" snaps Cassie.

David, though, looks nervous, stirs. "Cassie, can you take care of things?"

"I could if I had the safe combination." She turns to Andy Faragut. "He'll be out in a second." Andy stares at her a second or two longer than he needs to, but retreats.

David curls lethargically off the chair to kneel by the safe. He turns the knob once, twice, three times. Cassie steps closer, anticipating the satisfying click of an open safe, but David turns the knob, once, twice, three times again and then two more rounds. The safe remains closed. "Shit," he swears.

Cassie nearly kicks the desk in impatience. March 25 and October 26, Greek Independence Day and the anniversary of your grandfather's death, all the combinations are some variation on those numbers. How hard could it be to come up with something that will work?

"Let me try." He backs away and sits on the floor against the wall.

She kneels down and tries the most obvious combination first, three, twenty-five, ten, twenty-six. The door clicks open. She takes out the checkbook, hands it to him, stands, and kicks the bottom of his shoe. "Go."

David starts and stands up. "Cassie," he says and glances toward the door. "Cassie, you don't know what they're doing, how I'm being reeled in like a fish." His tall frame fills the office, and the top of his full hair nearly brushes the ceiling.

"What are you talking about?"

"My mother, she knows this family and . . ."

It's only a job, Cassie thinks. I'll never run this business, and I was a fool to think otherwise. "Why don't you just leave?"

He blinks at her, as if he doesn't understand the question, but then he shrugs his shoulders. "Where would I go?"

"Who's going?" asks Dodie.

"Going where?" interrupts Paul.

They stand on either side of David, their heads barely visible behind his wide shoulders, in a baffled triumvirate.

"Who the hell left all these lights on?" George's shout scatters them in different directions like struck pool balls.

Left alone, Cassie sits at the desk to gather up the undone delivery and tally sheets. She hears the doors at the loading dock open up as the trucks back in, but she focuses only on the numbers in front of her, on how many scallops and clams and to where.

Twenty minutes later she looks up at George in the doorway. "Why isn't David doing those?" he asks.

"I made coffee."

"Huh," he grunts and takes the completed sheets from her.

The photo of old Nicolas Cosmo, fists curled, glaring forward, stares down at her. Cassie reaches into the file cabinet, and pulls out her folder labeled "Future Growth." She's sure Nicolas Cosmo would have asked her eagerly about the Canadian distributors, quickly calculating gas, mileage, and the cost of a bigger fleet of trucks against the potential revenue of more customers and a new product. Nicolas Cosmo would have been a better boss than his conservative brother or his cautious son. But Nicolas Cosmo, fresh from Greece, with sketchy English and old-world ways, never would have hired her in the first place.

After an hour or so, George reappears in the doorway holding a cup of coffee. His hair is carefully combed, and his round shoulders and belly pull at the edges of a bright blue shirt. "You can go now."

Although Cassie is sure that old man Cosmo never thought for a second she had anything to do with that money being stolen, she is sure George considered it. It's funny. She knows so much about their business, they trust her with so many of the numbers that if she had wanted to steal money from

Cosmo's there were lots of ways to do it, ways they would never catch her. She could have doctored numbers from all over, intake from the clammers, checks from the restaurants, even coffee money.

She takes a deep breath. Andy Faragut has most likely mixed his old clams with his new ones by now, been paid, and left the building. "Sure, George," Cassie answers him. When George turns his back, she slips her own folder, "Future Growth," under her blue hooded sweatshirt and leaves.

Outside the refrigerated Quonset hut, the warm air is fragrant with the perfume of growing things. Her sweatshirt hangs heavy in the summer air, and Cassie quickly removes it and wraps it around the folder.

A dark sedan pulls under the maples and into the Cosmo lot. Cassie wonders if it's stealing to take a file you've put together yourself, if you had used your boss's paper and done it on the clock.

A young woman, a girl really, about her age emerges from the car. She is tall, with dark, full hair cascading down her back and pulled off her face with a wide, velvet headband dotted with rhinestones. The sun sparkles off the rhinestones like a crown or a halo. She is followed by an older couple, her parents perhaps, because both women share the same long, unmuscled legs.

Cassie turns toward her bike, her bulky package under her arm, but they take no notice of her. Before the tall stranger enters the Quonset hut, she smoothes down the front of her short green dress carefully like a person with all the time in the world, as her father and mother admire her, small smiles on their faces.

Then Cassie understands. This girl with her thin legs is tall, tall enough for David. The Cosmos are no fools. She wonders if they had to go all the way to Greece to find such delectable bait.

## June 30, 1971

The house is dark and the driveway empty. Maybe a street-light is out, but the backyard is pitch black, and Cassie fumbles to lean her bike against the side of the house.

Someone covers her mouth with a hand and grabs her from behind. "Why don't you watch yourself, for chrisakes, I could have been anyone." Mark crouches low and half drags, half maneuvers Cassie to the back of the yard, where he leans them both against the neighbor's wood-slat fence. When she breathes again, he smells bad, like beer and cigarettes and a musky sweat that's like nothing she's ever smelled before. Her shorts are damp, although she's not sure whether from fear or dew or her own sweat.

He shifts his head, scanning the yard. "It's freaky back here, all this brush, not even a real tree. Those tracks, Jesus, Cass, anything could come from there, anything from fucking any-where." He shifts his weight noiselessly. "This fence is shit, who knows what's on the other side?"

"It's the Bakers' backyard," Cassie whispers.

"Fuck!" he hisses. "You know that's not what I mean!" He turns to her. "You've got to learn to see it, feel it all around you, if you're gonna make it a day, don't you understand that?"

Even though it is a warm evening, Cassie is shaking, her skin raised in bumps. "I'm not sure I do."

"They go everywhere, everywhere we do, planting shit, you gotta get into their heads to protect yourself."

"Is that what you did?"

Mark trembles now, his whole body wracked with shaking.

"Lenny, why the fuck you turn your head around? I didn't mean it."

"Lenny turned his head around?" she asks.

"It was the last fucking thing he ever did."

"Did he turn around to look at you?"

"How the fuck did I know?" he shouts.

"How could you know?" she whispers.

"I was in their fucking heads! I should have known! He should have known! Shit!" These last consonants burst out harsh and loud, like an explosive. A light goes on in the Bakers' house next door. Mark jumps up, turns toward the fence. "Keep down," he hisses.

"But we're in Ipswich, Mark. There's nothing to be afraid of anymore." He holds her head down, and she's afraid to reach up and push his arm off her.

He sits back abruptly, and she sits up again. "You are! I don't fucking know where the fuck I am." He turns to her, grabs her arms tight. "What am I supposed to do now? Just turn it all off like a fucking switch?"

"Maybe it takes a little time." Her voice sneaks out, scared and unsure.

"Time," he says, bitterly.

"Why don't we go inside?"

Mark stands up.

"Where are you going?"

He walks away from her, toward the tracks.

She stands. "Are you carrying that gun? Please, Mark. You don't need a gun."

When he hits the tracks, he turns right and disappears.

She hears him running away from her. No matter how fast she is, one thing she has learned is not to trail him in the dark.

She leans against the fence, watches the quarter moon rise through the oak in the lot on the other side of the tracks. Her body is wet with sweat, and it is a few minutes before she breathes evenly again.

Once inside, Cassie searches Mark's letters. Somewhere in here he had described the butterflies in Vietnam, how big and colorful they were. She flips through some pages, starts to read. "Damn, Cass, I want to be calm like silk." This letter, from China Beach, was written when he had been sent out for a three-day leave. "But my nerves are alive and crawling, and I can't keep still. I might be out of the jungle, but my head's still in it. It's normal like this though, all the grunts repeat the same. The cong, man, those fuckers get under your skin, and there's no way you can ever wash them out." She sniffs the letter; it still smells faintly of coconut, of suntan oil.

What did he mean, her backyard is freaky? It's the same backyard it was when he left. Do they all come back like this? With freaky eyes that warp everything they see? The word freak lingers in her mind, wants to attach itself to Mark, but Cassie won't let that happen because a freak is someone you let go.

## July 1, 1971

Mr. Brooks wears a loose yellow tie that wraps around his neck like a bow on a present. Although the rest of his suit is tan, the sartorial effect is of a canary, maybe because the yellow is so bright, or maybe because Mr. Brooks is so thin that his hands fall out of his cuffs like the narrow feet of a bird on its perch.

Angie Richardson has been absent for three weeks. Rumor has it she met up with some old friends at a party, got back on the junk, and has been squatting in a basement in Gloucester. "Heroin's like that," Craig Murphy explained to Cassie even though she hadn't asked. "It's quick and dangerous and there's no turning back."

Angie's seat in the front remains empty, and Mr. Brooks has stopped asking after her at the beginning of each class. Cassie tries hard to concentrate, to ask the questions Angie used to ask, the ones that require multiple readings of the assignment, the ones that get Mr. Brooks off on a tangent or speaking in Greek.

The window shades, brittle yellowed paper, are half-lowered to keep out the summer light. A wet, chill breeze floats in off the water. Penelope is the topic.

"Why do we care about Penelope?" Mr. Brooks leans back against the front of his desk, arms over his chest, delicate crème-colored suede loafers crossed at the ankles. "For the nineteen years that Odysseus is gone, Penelope puts off her suitors. She promises to wed one of them only when she finishes her rug, which she weaves by day and then by night pulls apart. Work with no progress, the classic image of waiting." Fingertips together, he lifts his face toward the ceiling, and his yellow tie reflects onto his neck, like a buttercup held under the chin. "Upon his return, everyone in the household welcomes him but his own wife. She's cold, puts him off, tells the servants to make up a separate bed for him." He looks back out at the class. "Why?"

Cassie flips through the pages of the book. Although her waiting presence runs throughout the story, Penelope gets few lines and then only at the very end. Cassie remembers Penelope's kindness toward Helen, whom the Greeks had gone to retrieve from Troy. She looks down at the lines in which Penelope has only pity for Helen: "It surely was a god who spurred her act / of wantonness, who blinded her so that / she could not see what fate had brought to pass."

Poor Penelope, Cassie thinks, in her world any deception is possible. If the gods could lure Helen to run away with Paris, convince the Greeks to fight ten years to get her back, and then keep Odysseus from home for another ten years, then who is she to trust that the man standing in front of her is really her husband?

Cassie speaks up. "She doesn't trust her eyes, she thinks that the gods are tricking her like they tricked Helen into wanting Paris."

"They do trick her. Athena goes out of her way to make sure Odysseus looks taller, more robust; she even gives him a full head of hair just before he meets Penelope again." Mr. Brooks looks at Cassie. "But what is she afraid of?"

Cassie lightly touches her bruised eye. Penelope's fear, her fear of the stranger who says he is her husband, sits in her, heavy and squirming. "Maybe she's afraid she waited all that time for nothing."

Mr. Brooks lays his fingertips on the desk, two tents at his side. "Has she? After all, in the meantime Odysseus has had himself a really good time, seven years with Calypso and one with Circe, both goddesses of beauty and charm." He squints his eyes and smiles.

"No way!" shouts Craig Murphy. "They were witches! He and Penelope jump right into that tree bed! First chance they get!"

"Ah, the tree bed." Mr. Brooks stands up, and walks to the side of the classroom.

Cassie thinks of the bed, carved by Odysseus from a living tree with the roots still in the ground, the bed only he and Penelope and a trusted servant knew about, the bed that, once he mentions it, makes Penelope wrap her arms around his neck.

"Does that make up for his absence?" asks Mr. Brooks.

Cassie remembers the night on the beach with Mark before he left, the waves dragging across the pitted sand, the blue moonlight on the dunes, not a tree bed at all, merely a landscape that changes with the wind.

Mr. Brooks stands against the yellowed shades, and the muted summer light glows around him, sending his face into shadow. "Well then," he says. Outside, a car door slams, and the birds twitter high in the tree just by the open windows. "Perhaps we should all have a tree bed to come home to."

"Sure," snorts Bill from his usual spot in the back. "And then it only takes ten years before you're ready to sleep in it."

"We must conclude that Odysseus' wandering was no accident, then. Circe and Calypso were all part of the divine plan. And Penelope's waiting? What purpose did that serve?"

"Penelope gave the man his space," answers Bill. "And the man definitely needed his space."

## July 2, 1971

Cassie wakes to the clear, high tones of birds. Outside the kitchen window, pink streaks the sky; "the rosy fingers of dawn," Cassie reminds herself. Mr. Brooks would be proud.

She yawns, goes to the kitchen to check on the progress of Mark's gift. The screened caterpillar houses, their floors thick with detritus, smell earthy. One lone caterpillar chomps away at the remaining bit of food in the cage, a couple of partially eaten milkweed stems that lie in the black muck. This one might want another meal before it joins its dormant cousins, hanging hidden beneath gray skeins like vampires in their capes, upside down from the ceiling. Cassie remembers back to the first batch of butterflies. Wet and rolled, they'd rested at the edge of a coffee can, and Cassie had called Mark to come over, quick. She'd carried the cages outside in time for the first to step out into the air. By the time Mark arrived, number three fluttered over his head.

She eases the back door open slowly so as not to wake her father, but the birds are still going nuts over the arrival of the day as she steps outside. The steps, the ground, and the weeds glisten in chilly dew. She walks lightly toward a patch of milkweed in the back. Their pretty pink and white flowers are mostly gone, leaving only the plant and leaves. The green pods won't be visible for another month or so, and not until late fall will the dark gray case crack and release its fluffy seeded treasure. Cassie picks one or two nice-looking leaves and turns back to the house.

A lurch in her stomach nearly sends her reeling backward.

Someone sits, hollow eyed and ghostly, in her backyard. It's Mark. His military cut looks grown out to shaggy and disheveled. His T-shirt hangs off his shoulders, and his pants look too tight, too short even, and ride up over his ankles.

"I didn't mean to spook you."

"You don't spook me."

His hands dangle between his knees. "That's funny, 'cause I spook myself sometimes."

She walks slowly toward him and sits down next to him on the wet weeds. This close, he smells like sweat and booze and dirt. He has been up all night again, she thinks. He sways a bit, from drink or exhaustion or both. She holds up the leaves. "Only one left to feed," she says. "The rest are hanging."

"Really? Only about ten days, then, and they'll be ready to fly . . ." He looks at her face and stops. "What happened to you, Cass?" He reaches his hand a few inches from her cheek. She leans in to close the gap. His fingers touch her face, cold but gentle. "It looks like someone belted you." He asks this quizzically, as if not believing that could ever be the cause of her bruise.

Cassie hesitates. Given his outbursts, his unpredictability, and the gun in his car, it certainly would be safer to give him the freezer story. But she can't start lying to him now, as if he were not a person with enough value to merit the truth. "You did it," she says quickly, "when you were here, when you were asleep. You had some kind of nightmare and I went in and your arms flailed around and bingo, a shiner."

His shoulders shake and heave. "Fuck," he says. "Fuck, fuck, fuck, fuck." A gasping sound, similar to a sob, almost like retching, follows the shaking, and this is far worse than the anger or the coldness or the exhaustion or the drunkenness, these noises come from far away, from halfway across the world. "Look at you!" He stands up. "I'm taking you down with me!"

She stands too. "It's OK, Mark."

He turns on her, the anger back. "No, it is not OK!"

He looks wild and dirty and miserable. "Don't you see?"

"No, Mark . . ."

"Look at me, Cass!" He walks backward toward the tracks.

She knows that now she is really losing him, that up until this point he had been circling back to her. "It won't always be this way!" she calls.

"How do you know?"

"Because it can't be." She is crying, but she stands rooted to the ground. Touching him in this condition won't work, and she can't convince him that he is OK because it is so clear that he is not OK, that he is desperately not OK.

He is close to being out of the yard. "Cass, you know I'm not taking you down with me, you know I'd never do that."

She sees then that he still loves her, and the wonder at that quickly turns to worry that he will leave her, leave her because he thinks that he can only hurt her.

Mark turns and races zigzag down the tracks, his head shifting side to side, his movements jerky.

## July 3, 1971

Cassie rides along the twilight streets. Beyond the bright
cone of the streetlight, Bannon's, the bar with no frills, lurks
between shadows. A bone-thin woman with stringy blonde
hair zigzags her way out the door and up the sidewalk, her
arms threading the air as if she were treading water. She totters under the streetlight, eyes unfocused, face bloodless as
she lurches between the street and the sidewalk.

"Penny!"

Cassie looks back. Andy Faragut is half-running, half-lop-
ing along the sidewalk in their direction. "What the hell!
Penny!" He reaches her, tries to grab her wrist. Penny raises
her arms to weakly fend him off, a thin trickle of blood running down her arm to her wrist. What had Craig Murphy
from class said about heroin, that it was quick and dangerous? Andy takes her gently around the shoulders and pulls
her back toward the bar. Cassie thinks she knows who stole
the money from the safe and wonders why it didn't occur to
her before. Everybody said Andy has an expensive habit, but
it looks to Cassie as if the Cosmo clam money is really cours-
ing its way through the veins of his girlfriend.

## July 4, 1971

The morning breaks hot, like high summer.

Cassie, groggy and hungry, makes her way to the kitchen and sits down. On the counter, the Morton Salt Girl, lemon yellow dress under white umbrella, stands out from the navy blue label of the canister. Cassie picks up the salt, glances at the yellow dress and then at the wall behind it. She holds the canister up to the wall. The dress is yellow, but the wall looks white. She holds the canister up to the wall near the table and then against the wall next to the phone. The walls are white there too.

She sets the salt down. The kitchen has faded from yellow into ivory. Cassie reaches up to the pleated curtains that have hung over the sink window for as long as she can remember. The pattern bleached, there are no small flowers left, and the material is no longer any color at all. Cassie kneels up onto the counter to get a closer look. Dusty smells linger in the cotton, and small holes have formed along the creases.

Concealed between the worn outward facing pleats are narrow rectangles of bright yellow and whole, full flowers that once rambled the length of the curtains. Cassie flips over the material to look at the side that has faced out the window into the sun. That side is completely white.

She slides off the counter and onto the floor. The linoleum too could just as easily be called ivory as yellow. She runs her fingers over the squares, looking for the flecks of gold. These sparkles remain only under the counter, out of the path of traffic, at the edge of the squares.

"Did you lose something?" Frank Leahy steps through the back door with a carton of blueberries.

Cassie looks up. The second hand on the clock makes its staccato way around the face, counting the seconds lost as they fly by. She sits up and leans against the small cabinet door beneath the sink. "Dad, what color's the kitchen?"

"Yellow."

Maybe the morning sun, she thinks, has temporarily bled all the color from the kitchen, like a sleight of hand. "Yellow?"

"Your mother's favorite color," he answers. He gently slides the caterpillar boxes over to make room for the blueberries. "These are the first of the season." He kicks at her foot. "Get out of my way and I'll make us some pancakes, maybe some muffins."

From the table, Cassie peers through the screen at the still cocoons. In less than a week, they'll be butterflies.

Fifteen years is, after all, a long time to ask a paint to hold its color or cotton its pattern. What did she expect? Maybe if she had been more aware of her own world shifting, she might have been prepared for or at least expected changes in Mark. To expect him to remain the same after a year away as a soldier, to expect anything to remain the same, frozen, she sees now, is a mistake.

Her father hums. Cassie looks up, suspicious. "Who brought you those berries?"

"I thought I'd go down later and watch the parade," he answers.

Cassie remembers a Fourth of July parade many years ago. Her mother had only been gone a matter of months, and Cassie had not yet given up the hope that she would return. On that day the dawn sky was gray, low, and close, and the wet lawn soaked through the bed blanket she had wrapped around herself. She was waiting for the red convertible with a gold star on its door. Cassie doesn't remember when it was that her mother had told her that the ladies riding on the Fourth of July in the red convertibles with stars on their doors were mothers who had lost their children. But, wrapped in her blanket, she had been sure that the red car would come by carrying her lost mother, along with the other mothers who had lost their children. What she remembers now most clearly is her father's distress, brusque as the cold on the blanket, when he found her wrapped in her bedding on the main street two blocks from home, at close to dawn. He had swooped her up, and she had cried, "I'm waiting for Mommy!"

Only years later did she learn that those women in the parade were gold-star mothers, women whose sons were dead, killed in World War II, that the mothers had lost their children, but that they weren't riding in the parade in hopes to find them.

Cassie wonders if her father remembers the incident, but something about the happy way he measures the coffee keeps her quiet.

By eleven, the temperature is already over eighty degrees and the sun beams down from a blue and brilliant cloudless sky. A slight breeze barely lifts the flags that droop from the neighbors' poles or hang listlessly from their front porches or windows. A small explosion of cherry bombs ignites a few streets over, signaling the holiday.

Cassie and Frank Leahy walk a few blocks over to catch the parade along its last leg. The parade route is loosely lined with spectators, some in lawn chairs and some with baby carriages. The high school marching band announces itself from a distance, while two little boys wave small flags and run crazy back and forth across the wide, black street at their approach.

The marchers wear bright white, orange, and black uniforms;

the flag girls spin the poles, and the majorettes, sparkly and new because they've always bought their own uniforms, hold their batons high up against their shoulder like weapons until a break in the action when they fling them in the air in unison. One of the girls, thick, dark hair running down her back, looks like her old friend Sue Wocjik, and Cassie stands on her toes to call out to her before she remembers that Sue would have graduated last year.

Following the band, a trim middle-aged man in a neat combat green suit, red stripes on his arms, holds the American flag, and another uniformed man carries the flag of Massachusetts to lead an Army contingent. Then come the crisp Marines, the Navy in their bright white pants, the Air Force with their smart blue caps, and marching as a group, the men from World War I in their spats and ironed caps, trailed by the Boy Scouts and smaller Cub Scouts. Here Cassie spots Paul Harris, Mark's little nephew, marching in a blue shirt and yellow tie. None of the men marching look young enough to have been in Vietnam. She wonders when that happens, when people who have been soldiers decide to put their uniforms on and march again. Spooky Wilson, for one, never marched in any parade Cassie can remember.

Today only one small, gray-haired woman, wearing a long-sleeve blue dress, rides in the back of the gold-star convertible. She waves at the crowd as people clap.

Why a gold star? Why not a teardrop, or a skull? Cassie steps back out of the sun. The mother must be hot in that heavy dress, and hopefully someone will have a cold drink for her at the end of the route, for her trouble.

Next come a police car, its light flashing blue and soundless, and the fire truck. At the sight of the fire truck, the children scream and rush from the sidelines to gather up the Tootsie Rolls and Smarties and lollipops thrown from the back. The truck's piercing alarm and flashing red light signal the end of the parade.

In the candy melee behind her, Frank Leahy is deep in conversation with a sergeant, about a thirty-two-inch striper he caught last summer. This story is a long one, so Cassie heads off.

Cassie peeks into the cave of the living room, an oasis of dark in this overbright July day, when her dad turns on the TV and settles into his chair. He refuses to take the boat out on this holiday, too busy, he claims.

A whirring sounds from the room. "Come on and sit in front of the fan," says her father, "and watch the ballgame with me."

"Lonborg's a bum!" she answers, picking on this season's favorite pitcher.

"A bum with a job."

Cassie hands her dad a bottle of Blue Ribbon, sinks into the couch. "You need the car tonight?"

"You want me to drop you somewhere?"

So, she registers, her dad is going out. Teri mentioned fireworks in Gloucester, and Stu is eager to show off Nina's work on his new car. She should probably make some phone calls, but she doesn't want to leave her chair. On another Fourth of July, she and Mark would have spent the day on the beach or out on his dad's whaler or her dad's outboard, and then watched some fireworks together, on the grass, in the dark under explosions of color and noise. Cassie feels the pulse of sadness, a kind of grief, and she's too tired to shoo it away, too tired to wipe away the tears that fall down her face. "Nah," she answers her dad.

Cassie watches the crowd at Fenway rise for a long hit ball that bounces off the top of the wall, and then she closes her eyes. The air is cooler in here and the dark soothing.

As Cassie rinses the soapy dinner dishes, she hears the phone ring over the rush of water from her dad in the shower. Expecting Teri she picks up, fights to keep hold of the wet receiver, and leans against the wall.

"Cassandra?" says Mr. Pinter, peremptory and commanding. "I need to speak with Teri."

The shower turns off in the bathroom.

"She isn't here." Even in the soft early evening sun, the kitchen doesn't look yellow. Cassie bites her lip.

Mrs. Pinter gets on the phone. "Hello, Cassie," she says with a sticky pretense at warm and confidential. If I were a spider, Cassie thinks, she would make me curl my legs up and fold into a ball.

"Hello, Mrs. Pinter."

"We need to speak with Teri."

"But she's not here." Cassie glances at the clock over the stove, the most accurate in the house. It reads after seven.

"Well." Mrs. Pinter takes a deep breath. Cassie pictures her drumming her fingernails on her spotless counter. "She left here ten minutes ago and we're sure she was on her way to your house."

Teri would have called me before now, Cassie thinks, if she had really wanted to go to the fireworks. She feels an instinctive need to cover tracks for her friend. "She and Nina . . ." she begins.

"Nina?" Mrs. Pinter interrupts. "You know where Nina is?"

"Are you looking for Nina?" Cassie asks, as lightly as she can.

Mr. Pinter is back on the phone. "Cassie, if you know where Nina is, it is imperative that you tell us." His peremptory tone commands a sense of responsibility, a respect for authority, but all it triggers in Cassie is distrust. Somewhere a door slams, and Cassie wonders whether one Pinter parent will keep her on the phone while the other drives here to question her in person or to wait for Teri. Cassie wipes her soapy hands on her shorts, carefully transferring the receiver from one hand to the other. She is tired of waiting for bad things to happen. "Teri and Nina are heading into Boston to see the fireworks, that's all I know Mr. Pinter," she lies. "I'm sorry I can't help you anymore." She lays down the receiver as quietly as possible so it will not feel as if she is hanging up on them. "Dad!" She walks into the hallway. "Dad! I'm going now!"

Frank Leahy opens the bathroom door and a flood of steam rolls into the already hot hall. Face flushed, he's wearing a neat checkered shirt and smells of aftershave. "Where?"

She smiles. "I should ask you that question."

He's flustered, and she takes the advantage. She kisses him on the cheek. "I'm going to the fireworks Dad, I'll see you later."

Cassie slips out the back door before he can answer or before one of the Pinter parents calls back, and jogs quickly down the driveway. Sure the Pinters said that Teri was on her way, but why wouldn't she call herself to say so? Cassie hesitates behind the neighbor's oak tree before she sets out along the sidewalk. The summer sun is still bright over the horizon as if it will never set, and Cassie thinks of the cemetery that runs up the hill across from White's Garage, and of her mother's grave high on that hill with its view of the ocean. She increases her pace.

In just a minute or two, Teri pulls up in Mr. Pinter's car. "Get in!"

The car is air conditioned and freezing, and Cassie huddles in the front seat rubbing her arms up and down, her toes curled in her rubber flip-flops.

"Cass, did you sleep in those clothes?"

Cassie looks down at herself. She is wearing the same tank top, cutoff shorts, and flip-flops she has had on all day. "Can't we turn this off and open some windows?"

"Sorry, my dad likes it frigid." Teri flips a few knobs. "I should have called, but I had to leave. My parents got a phone call from Nina's parents. It turns out that she was supposed to meet her uncle in Italy, but she sold her plane ticket and never showed up at the airport."

"So, the police found her?"

"No. Apparently this kind of thing has happened before so they hired a private detective."

Cassie remembers how Nina zeroed in like a target on the black eye Mark had given her, how she offered, not sympathy, but maybe witness, behind the lens of her camera. "Who is she running from? Her uncle?"

Teri shrugs. "She withdrew some money in Boston, that's how they found her. This detective did this whole search of her regular friends, you know, who is in this area, and then they widened it to classes she took, and that's how they found me."

Nina came to Teri then, thinks Cassie, because they weren't really that close, because she didn't want to leave a trail. "She gambled then, when she went to get money to buy Stu's paints."

"Gambled and lost." Teri slows down at the yield. "Look! There's Stu's bike at White's!" She pulls into the gas station, puts the car in park. "Cass, Nina is running from something. I know you're not overly fond of her and I admit she is hard to take sometimes, but think about it. If it scares Nina, then it's probably worth running from."

Stu, holding a license plate up to his forehead to shield his face against the sun, appears at the side of the car. "I hope you guys don't need gas 'cause it's a bitch to open the pumps after hours." A bottle rocket, soft swoop followed by a loud crack, flies off in the A&P lot across the road, its echoes tracing along the empty streets.

Either Teri doesn't notice his richly bloodshot eyes, or she chooses to ignore them. "Stu, what happened to Nina?"

He laughs. "What happened to her? I don't know. But she turned out all right, don't you think?"

"Where is she now, Stu?" says Cassie, impatient with his

banter. "Teri's got news for her."

"She's putting the finishing touches on the car, it looks unbelievable, just like an artist, you gotta come see it. I just stopped by for some plates so we could take it for a ride."

"Let's go take a look," says Teri, starting up the engine.

"Hey, Cass," adds Stu, looking across Teri to her, "Mark's there too, been helping out some."

At the mention of his name, a grip of panic and uncertainty threatens to scare her out of herself. "Wait for me," she says. She pushes open the car door, sprints across the street, through the open arch of the black metal gate that guards the graveyard, and up the worn-thin stone steps, two, then three at a time. As she climbs, the sounds of the town below, cherry bombs, car engines, a barking dog, swell out behind her and grow fainter as she distances herself from them. Near the top of the hill she stops to catch her breath. Here the graves are newer and farther apart, and the light blue of the ocean in the early evening shimmers on the horizon. She finds her mother's grave quickly and kneels before it: "Katharine Flynn Leahy, 1926-1956," and written along the top, "Thy Will Be Done."

She closes her eyes. Sun through yellow curtains, a cracking egg, and the press of her mother's hug, this is what she remembers. But the feeling of being held and lifted up, this never leaves her, and this she knows is her mother. Dad's got a date, she tells her, he was all clean and smelled good.

She rubs her palms over the grass above the grave to make her thoughts real, stands, and runs back down the stone steps. Thy will be done, thy will be done, thy will be done, she repeats.

Teri and Stu watch after her as she re-crosses the street and sits back in the front seat next to Teri. "Let's go," she tells them. "I'm ready."

Stu's motorcycle vanishes quickly and is parked and quiet

by the time Teri and Cassie pull up to the Camineau lawn. Mark's car is nowhere in sight.

In the airless backyard, the slanted early evening light, as if through stained glass, glows green and gold through the trees and grass and weeds.

Nina, red in the face as if from sunburn, her hair tousled, leans against a large rock, her knees up. Gravity pulls her short skirt off her thighs, revealing most of her legs and a good portion of her underwear.

Nina swallows the last of a beer and tosses the can aside. "We'd offer you one," she says, "but we're waiting for reinforcements."

"What reinforcements?" asks Cassie.

"Come on, you gotta see the car," says Stu.

Nina fishes around in a large red, green, and tan striped woven bag. "What the hell," she mutters. Almost regal in her dissipation, nothing about her invites shared confidences.

Cassie walks over to Stu's Eldorado. Painted on the hood in intricate greens and blues is a huge dragon's head with a force of red and orange flames streaming out of the sides of its open mouth. But nothing is just one color; the colors swarm together like water, as if the dragon is swimming over the roof of the car. Every brush stroke has bits of gold or purple or brown or different shades of blues and greens. The dragon's eyes, a mosaic of yellow, pierce through the dark-colored head in a fierce stare and follow Cassie as she makes her way around the sides.

"Isn't it wild?" asks Stu.

"Wild?" says Cassie. "This thing's alive."

"We've gotta tell her about her parents," says Teri. She glances at Nina, who tries to light a joint with a failing lighter.

She regards the small flame cupped in her palm. "It isn't finished."

"This is fantastic, Nina," says Cassie. "It's beautiful." Maybe Nina smiles, or maybe she's just trying to suck more air through her joint.

"Gotta tell her what?" asks Stu.

"Nina's parents are looking for her, she's been running," whispers Teri. "They hired a private detective."

Mark appears from around the corner, a case of beer on his shoulder. His hair is disheveled, and he's wearing some kind of baggy, long army green pants, with a T-shirt that has lost most of its color in the wash. "Reinforcements!" he calls out. He drops the case on the scrubby grass, takes out a beer, and pops off the top with an opener hanging from a chain off his belt loop. He takes a long drink and then waves his bottle at the crowd. "Be my guest," he says as he avoids looking directly at any of them.

Cassie can tell it's an act; tightness stiffens his mouth and shoulders, his eyes dart the circumference of the yard. Mark isn't near drunk yet.

He reaches down for a beer, pops the top for her, hands it over, saying nothing. It tastes warm, unpleasant and bitter.

Teri takes two beers and brings one over to Nina. As she hands it to her, Teri kneels down and talks in a low voice, her back screening Nina's face.

Stu considers them with a glance, opens the Eldorado, and turns on the radio. The loud music fills the empty yard and makes it impossible for any conversation at less than a shout.

Cassie can only guess that Teri's delivered the news that Nina's parents are circling in on her, but Nina remains fixed against the rock.

The light leaves the sky in a shifting tableau of color into darkness, and the case of beer is drunk. Stu makes himself at home in the front seat of his magnificent car. Cassie barely manages two bottles, which she regrets as she feels the clarity of her anger dissipate into the alcohol. Teri, a few feet to her right, leans against a rock like a sentry, her untouched beer by her side, while Mark pops one beer after another.

At some point "Star Spangled Banner" comes on. Hendrix's guitar screams into the empty night and balances on the stillness of its own vibrations before it streaks off into the dark, sharp and insistent.

Someone flicks the back lights on. That creepy Mrs. Camineau, Cassie thinks, she's been home the whole time.

In the glare, Nina gets to her feet.

Stu turns off the radio, steps from the car into the harsh light, and wipes the sweat off his forehead with the back of his hand. "That sure is some crazy shit."

"I used to love fireworks when I was little," says Nina. "All the booms felt like they exploded inside me, and all the bright colors that took over the sky, it was like I could crawl into them and disappear. I could never paint them, though, not the way they are."

Teri stands. "Sounds good, let's go."

Nina stands with her. "OK."

She lifts up her bag. Cassie wonders if she thought to bring her cash, if she knew she had to run tonight, or if she's going back to the Pinter's house after all.

"We can take my car," says Stu.

"Stu!" snaps Nina, who despite her disheveled appearance gives orders with surprising specificity. "That paint has to set, I told you, for seventy-two hours. You can't mess with shit like that. And if it rains, you need to cover it with that tarp!"

Cassie watches Mark staring at the dragon as his fingers caress the hood.

The group stumbles back toward the front yard. Stu trips over something, swears. "Hey," he shouts, "I'll get my bike."

"No!" Teri says. Her voice is as sharp as a piece of glass. "I mean," she dulls her edge, "I can drive. I've got my dad's car." She looks at Stu. "It's got a brand new eighty-eight in it."

Cassie smiles. Only Teri could pull stuff like that out of nowhere.

Mark opens his passenger door, looks at Cassie, and then gets in the driver's seat and starts the engine.

"Come on, Nina." Stu urges her toward Teri's car. But she hesitates, glances toward Mark.

Cassie sees that Nina would get into any car that will take her. Mark, however, for the first time all night, looks at Cassie, as if to say how could anyone else ever sit in the front seat of his car? She remembers the look he gave her at the airport, when he got on Stu's bike. Mark had issued no invitation but everyone there expected her to follow along, to do whatever he wanted. What if what he wanted was messed up?

Cassie calls back to Teri, "We'll follow you," and with a heavy reluctance gets in and closes the door behind her.

Mark smells like hard sweat and drinking. As he peers into the night, his movements are slack, a lot of his habitual tenseness drunk away.

He drives slowly. The town is quiet. When the streetlights run out and her eyes adjust to the dark, windy roads to Gloucester, Cassie remembers the details of Mark's letters: the places, Mekong, Binh Hoa, Saigon, the names, Lenny, Blipboy, Tarbox, the leeches, the bugs, the foot rot, the smell, the sadness, the horror. If he has already told her all there is to tell, why does he act like she's such a stranger to him?

Cassie is angry that he has spent the last two hours ignoring her, angry that his return has been no return at all.

Teri's taillights flicker in the distance. "Where are you going?"

He looks at her, surprised. "Aren't we going to the fireworks?"

The road curves into the night, under the full summer trees, around the small hills and rocky outcroppings left by glaciers ten thousand years ago, and past the darkened houses set back off the street.

"Why do you have that gun?"

His hands tighten on the steering wheel.

"You can't have that gun, Mark. You know you can't handle it."

He turns to stare at her. "Mark, the road . . ."

He thumps the steering wheel with his fist, and the car swerves to the right and back again.

Cassie no longer cares how angry she makes him, convinced that he would never harm her. "You don't need the gun here."

"They blew up! They all looked back at me and they blew up! You happy now?"

Cassie pictures Mark, with the radio and so at the back of the line, his friends in front, then his friends gone. It was horrible. "It wasn't your fault."

"In a million pieces." He says this quietly, but waves of tenseness radiate around him.

She thinks of Odysseus traveling, telling his stories for years before he could come home. Those Greeks were wise; they had probably seen enough of war to know how to deal with its aftermath.

Up ahead, Teri's car has turned into the parking lot at the Richdale's. Cassie points, "In here, Mark." He pulls into the lot, and then, leaving the engine running, he jumps out of the car and paces, twisting from side to side, stiff and mechanical. Cassie follows.

Stu, standing by Teri outside the car, calls to them. "Nina had to use the restroom."

Somewhere in the distance a series of bottle rockets explodes. Mark leaps toward Cassie, pulls her to the ground, and then rolls a turn or two with her. She barely gathers herself from the fall when Mark is moving forward. He half crouches, half crawls to the car. His head darts from side to side as he reaches into the open passenger window, and pulls out his gun.

"Holy shit!" says Stu.

Cassie scrambles back to her feet. Another round of rockets

ignites in ear-piercing sequence. Mark crouches, turns toward the sound, and fires into the woods.

"Mark, please!" yells Cassie.

At the convenience store, the clerk appears at the glass door and retreats. Nina runs out seconds after. "We gotta go, cops on the way, come on."

"Mark," shouts Cassie again, "we gotta go."

Mark drops his arm but Cassie can see he is shaking, fighting with himself. He doesn't want to let go of the gun. She walks toward him. In the light breeze of the warm evening, Mark reeks of an acrid stench unlike normal sweat. "It's just fireworks," she says. "You've got to get rid of the gun."

"I'm not joking," says Nina. "That kid's in there calling the cops."

Cassie is nearly to Mark. "The cops are gonna come soon."

Mark hesitates.

"Cass," hisses Stu, "we've got to get him out of here now!"

Cassie touches his arm, "Mark, please." He drops his arm to the side, his face uncertain.

Another burst of cherry bombs goes off. Mark grabs her and pulls her with him behind the closest boulder. In the quiet second that follows, he puts his hands over his head and crouches into a tight ball. The gun lies by his feet.

He is shaking. "Jesusjesusjesus," he mutters, "I coulda killed someone." The blue moonlight makes his skin look like a thin veil over his body, and for a flash Cassie thinks of Teri and Nina's anatomy class. She sees the bones beneath: the sockets where his eyes should be, the double bones of the lower arms as they bend around his empty jaw, his ribs rounding out a hollow space in the middle. Then he is Mark again, brown hair askew, camouflage pants, old T-shirt. Cassie starts to cry. Please, please, please, she prays, please let me help him.

She thinks of her mother, and can only recollect a blurry face and soft brown hair, a voice saying to her, "Shh, shh, Cassandra. Eggs break. Things break."

"Mark, let's get out of here." She kicks the gun to the side.

"You don't belong with me."

"Please, Mark . . ."

"No!"

Cassie stands and turns to Stu and Teri and Nina, who wait by Teri's car. "He won't go with me!" she says wildly. "He won't go with me!"

Nina jogs toward them. "I got an idea." Despite her hair wild around her head and her short skirt, she stands solidly on her tall plastic sandals, her large bag firm on her shoulder. "I'll take him. I need to get out of here."

"Do it," says Stu, "the cops will be here."

She knows Nina is right, that there is no choice. The last thing Mark needs is the cops on his tail. Cassie wastes no time. She puts her arm around Mark's shoulders, draws him close, puts her mouth on his ear. He shudders. "Shh," she whispers, "shh."

"I can't take you with me where I'm going."

"You won't. I'm not going with you."

Stu helps Cassie maneuver him to the passenger seat as Nina gets behind the wheel. She quickly turns the car out of the lot and onto the street. As she takes off toward the highway, she waves her fingers out the open window, in a brief sort of goodbye.

Stu grabs Cassie by the shoulders. "We gotta go." They race toward the car. Teri, car already started, takes off in the opposite direction from Nina and Mark.

They have driven just a few yards when Cassie cries out, "Wait, we've got to go back, we can't just leave that gun there. What if they trace it back to Mark?"

"Don't worry," says Teri.

"Don't worry about that," says Stu.

"What do you mean?"

Teri glances in the rearview mirror. "I've got it under control."

"What's that supposed to mean?"

"She's got it," says Stu, "she got it when you were talking to Mark."

Cassie looks at Teri, tense behind the wheel of her father's Olds, going above the speed limit, but not by too much. She could have let Nina's parents find Nina, but she didn't. She could have taken off when Mark fired the gun, left Mark or Cassie or Stu for the cops to find, but if she even considered it, no one knew. She could have taken off a thousand times, but she didn't. Of all of them, medical school on the horizon, she was the one with the most to lose. "Teri," Cassie begins, "thank . . ."

"Don't you breathe a word of this to anyone," she interrupts. "We'll just drop it in the creek and no one will find it for ages."

Cassie closes her eyes and leans back against the plush seat. How far would Nina take him? How far would they go together? How long would it be until he returns? She shakes her head, no, I can't start asking that question.

Another small rocket explodes above them. Cassie wonders if Mark heard it, if he is cowering in the front seat. Will Nina be able to calm him? With a jolt she remembers, it was Circe who comforted Odysseus, not Penelope. By the time Penelope saw him, Odysseus had spent years with the witches, Circe and Calypso.

"Damn," says Stu, "damn. She must have spent a fortune on those paints. Each tube was like, ten bucks and she bought about thirty of them."

"She had a lot of money," says Teri. "I think she was probably carrying cash in that bag of hers."

No one mentions Mark, not because no one is thinking of him, but because they haven't got the vocabulary to explain the alien creature he has become, sent away from home to participate in horror, and then dropped back off without instructions, like a newborn baby.

It's after two in the morning, but the lights are on in the Leahy kitchen where Frank Leahy nurses a cup of ice coffee.

"Dad, what are you still doing up?"

"Waiting for you."

She sits.

She remembers the first time she kissed Mark. They sat on the back steps as an orange butterfly with black markings crawled to the top of a blue coffee can, waiting for its wings to dry. It perched on the edge of the can on its black toes, then fluttered away, straight and low to the ground and then high up, toward the trees. Then, wordless, she'd turned to find herself kissed, and she'd kissed him back as if it was what they both knew would happen.

They released twenty-two monarchs that summer, until Mark got his draft notice and the sun was too low and the air too cold to lay eggs.

She looks at the silent, gray cocoons. They would be monarchs soon, culled from milkweed plants, fed the leaves, and then let go.

"How was your date, Dad?"

He smiles. "Jesus," he says, "you're a funny one. You look like hell and you're asking me the questions. Just like your mother."

Cassie runs her fingers through her dirty hair, and then puts her elbows on the table to cradle her head. She looks at her father. "I miss her, Dad," she says finally. "I miss her a lot."

Frank Leahy looks at his daughter, and then at the ice in his coffee. "I do too," he answers her. "I do too."

## July 6, 1971

Early in the morning, Cassie rides to work under a perfect blue sky. The maples in the lot have lost their reddish tinge and bloom full and green, and the slight scent of wild honeysuckle growing on the back fence drifts toward her.

Inside, she is struck by the cold gloom of the place. No one is in the office, but when she sees that the coffee is started, her heart jumps a beat. The old man must be here, he is the only person other than Cassie who consistently makes the coffee. This will be easier than she anticipated to tell them who she thinks stole the money from the safe.

At the shuckers' station, a dozen women sit hunched over pails, their sporadic conversation lost in the high ceiling and drone of the refrigeration. It's low tide now, so the clammers won't be in for another three hours, but the delivery trucks will be loading up soon. Cassie knows the rhythm of this place like she knows the rhythm of her own home. Teri might have looked down on the work, but Cassie knows she has learned a lot here, and been given more responsibility in the gap that Cosmo's age and David's turn at college created.

She finds him by the cranky freezer, with a measuring tape. Today the old man really does look old. His white hair has grown sparse over the last year or so, and his shoulders a little hunched. He turns at her approach. "Cassie, just hold this end for me." He hands her the tape, the ends fumbling between his fingers. "I need to know what size I can order to fit in this spot. The guy had some extras I can get at a discount if I can fit them in."

Cassie smiles. If there was a deal to be found, old man Cosmo would sniff it out. She takes the tape and they measure the space. "You want me to write this down?" she asks.

"Nah. We'll remember."

When they finish, Cassie begins before she loses her nerve. Although she has no proof and the money's long spent, she has to tell the old man about Andy Faragut and his girlfriend's heroin addiction. "I've got something to tell you. I think I know who might have taken the money."

He holds up his hand. "You talk to George about that, OK?"

"OK," she says, surprised.

"Cassie," he continues, "you put in good time here. Some crazy took that money."

She looks at him, confused. Something's on his mind.

"So, tell me, when's the wedding?" he asks.

"Wedding? I'm not the one getting married."

Cosmo squints his eyes in disappointment. He wants to usher her from Cosmo Shellfish to a secure future as a wife.

"I'm going away to school," she says, the plans forming as she speaks. "All right?"

He sighs, pats her on the arm. "You're a worker, and we can always use a worker around here."

She nods. "I'll go do the sheets." Back in the office, she looks at the picture of the young Cosmo and his brother Nicolas Cosmo, founders of Cosmo Shellfish, hands down, fingers curled, staring at the future in front of the just-delivered Quonset hut. They left their country, their language, their family to come here; and once you left that little village in Sparta you didn't expect to return. Sure, prosperity and opportunity were why you came here, but only if poverty or war was why you left. She touches the photo with the tips of her fingers. They didn't know what was going to happen next, either.

## July 12, 1971

Cassie gets a postcard in the mail, a picture of the Badlands of North Dakota. There is no message, but she recognizes the handwriting in her name and address. She slips the card into her back pocket.

She laces on her new sneakers and steps onto the track. The gravel crunches in satisfaction. The shoes are weightless, almost buoyant. I'm going to run until I drop, she tells herself, like the first marathon, until my legs are jelly and my heart gives out.

She takes the track. She's gained endurance since that first hesitant run a few weeks ago. These are legs with power and she uses them to push around each turn without any rest on the straightaway. Her arms are strong from her years of lifting bushels at Cosmo and she uses them, too, to pull herself along, like climbing a rope out of water. The clear point of dissolution, when her oxygen production can't keep up with her output, when her muscles are no longer crisp and her lungs no longer efficient, this point takes longer and longer to reach, and this Cassie takes as progress.

Even then, tired out, she doesn't stop, but merely slows to walk several times around the track, her breath in soft heaves. Fatigue falls off her with her sweat, until she allows herself to collapse onto the ground.

On the grass, tickly and pungent and soft, she remembers the details as they roll over her. Maybe in seven years, when each of her body's cells has died and been replaced, these memories will be gone too, or maybe she will continually recreate them, the memories embedded like DNA in every new cell.

She remembers that swimming into the dark on a night-time beach was like swimming into trust.

She remembers running over the sand, through the hot late summer air, diving into the warm, resistant water, resurfacing, and looking back for Mark. The moon was gibbous, low-slung sliver, and she heard the glide of the waves over the sand, when he popped up behind her. His body was slippery and warm and his mouth was open and wet, and she felt as if every moment she had lived up until that very second had been solely to deliver her to that place, where she and Mark could release themselves to each other, to the water that swallowed them, and to the sky that offered cover, but not shelter.

When the water felt cold, they went back to their clothes. Mark took his shirt and rubbed the drops off Cassie, and she let him, and then she took his head in her hands and kissed his face, which was salty like the ocean, and he said, "I don't want to go. Cass, don't let me go."

Cassie sits up. Her face is wet with grief. She is not Penelope and life doesn't offer up a series of people to replace those that you've lost. Maybe sometimes patience is rewarded by love and sacrifice by glory, but each loss is permanent.

## November 1, 1971

The wind is erratic, fresh and cold, and the weeds in the abandoned lot are brittle and rattle like bones. Cassie passes by the overgrown patch on her way to the science lab, and something catches her eye.

She climbs over the mesh of sticks to a stand of strong-stemmed weeds with a series of symmetrical brown sacs. She tears a dried pouch open and releases the fluffy white parachutes of hanging brown seeds. Some of the tiny silken strands stick to her fingers, but most of them take bold flight in the chill gusts.

She waits until all the sacs are broken, their messengers scattered before she runs the block to be on time for her biology lab.

Inside, her hands are red and pulsing in the warmth as she takes out her notebook and scrambles out of her heavy coat.

Her lab partner watches as she manages to take a seat seconds before the professor arrives. "Hey," he whispers to her. He reaches over, lightly pulls something out of her hair, and sits back.

"It's a . . ." she starts to tell him.

He holds the seed between his fingers, softly rubs the cottony fibers. "I know what it is," he smiles. "It's butterfly food."

This time of year the marshes are thin, shades of brown sharp against a deep fall sky. Bare in places, up pop the islands of mud and weeds and roots that support them. Soon, the marsh will be gray, muted into a winter sky, and the reeds will shrink back into the ice and cold, looking as if nothing will ever grow there again. Surrounded as she is now by sidewalks and concrete buildings and traffic, the ocean feels far away, as if it never existed, except for the dream she has sometimes just before she falls asleep, the one where she's walking out of the shallow waves, onto the hot sand, and as the wind blows her hair in her eyes, she turns her face toward someone who is waiting for her, just out of sight.

# ACKNOWLEDGMENTS

I have been blessed – the list of all the people who have been generous with their time and expertise as I've written and marketed this book would be longer than the story itself. My heartfelt thanks to all of you who gave me the encouragement to liberate my writing from my desk drawer.

Thank you to those who patiently read drafts and offered suggestions: Kitty Babakian, Peter Bell, Edward DeAngelo, Amy Forman, Susan Golden, Illana Katz, Ruthann Marston and especially to Sally Brady.

Thank you to my peerless writing group: Maragaret Eckman, who doubled up as copy editor, Lana Barrett Owens and Laura Smith.

Thank you to Dean Papademetriou, who took a chance with this book.

And, last but never least, thank you to Russell, without whom none of this would be possible.

# QUESTIONS AND TOPICS FOR DISCUSSION

1. Post traumatic stress disorder (PTSD) wasn't labeled and defined until the mid-nineteen-seventies, and even then it took several years before the term came into general use and understanding. How do you think that the characters in this story could have benefited from knowing what PTSD is? Do you think more is being done today to recognize and treat this disorder in returning veterans?

2. Were you surprised by Mark's reception at Logan Airport? Would you be surprised to learn that such receptions became common, especially toward the end of the Viet Nam War? How has our ability to learn to separate the dedication of the soldier from the policies of the government changed since the Viet Nam era?

3. What did you think of Bill Leahy? How would you describe the relationship between Cassie and her father?

4. How is the Greek immigrant community conveyed in the story? In what way is Cassie both an insider and an outsider in the Cosmo world? How does the theft contribute to Cassie's understanding of her role? How is David Cosmo trapped in a way that his grandfather wasn't?

5.  Attitudes toward the role of woman have changed since 1971. How are they reflected in the novel – in, for example, Teri's attitude toward her work or Cassie's trip to the shoe store?

6.  How do the scenes in Mr. Brook's classroom and the discussion of Homer's *The Odyssey* add to the reader's understanding of the historical context of the returning-from-war story, that every war has returning veterans who have difficulty coming home?

7.  How would you describe Nina? Do you know any people like her? What role does Nina play in Mark's final decision?

8.  The U.S. government employed various methods for drafting soldiers during the Viet Nam War, but luck and connections played a huge role in whether a person served in combat or not. Do you think Stu fully understands how Mark's time in combat cuts him off from those who haven't shared the same experience?

9.  Discuss the nature of Cassie's friendship with Teri and with Stu. How do these friends offer different kinds of support for her?

10.  How should Cassie have interpreted Mark's last letter home to her, in which he said, "You don't owe me anything?" Could Cassie have done anything to change the outcome of the story?

11.  How does the natural cycle of the monarch butterfly and the milkweed plant serve to remind readers about the balance of relationships? Or about the na-

ture of change and growth?

12. Did you expect the story to end the way it does?
What will Mark do next? What would have been an
alternative ending?